AN OLD BLUE CORPSE

A New Haven Mystery

John Morton Blum

PublishAmerica
Baltimore

First printing

ISBN: 1-4137-5061-3
PUBLISHED BY PUBLISHAMERICA, LLLP
www.publishamerica.com
Baltimore

Printed in the United States of America

Author's note:

Yale University is of course a real university, and a great one, but the characters, incidents and situations in this book are imaginary and have no relation to any person or actual event. Readers who know Yale and New Haven will recognize that I have taken some small liberties with the geography and architecture of both town and campus.

For Abigail, con amore,
because she asked for it.

Acknowledgments

Dr. Stephen G. Waxman generously provided me with some informal instruction about poisons. Henry Chauncey, Jr., described the arrangement of furniture in the office of the secretary of the university. I am grateful to both of them. Neither is in the least responsible for any errors I may then have made in using the information I received.

៷   ៚

PROLOGUE: ISABEL

She was fat, so fat she waddled when she walked. And she was idiosyncratic. In her tote she carried an unopened box of good chocolate to her desk every day, and she nibbled her way through the box before she left in the late afternoon. Mad for jewelry, she wore rings on the middle fingers of her left hand. Two had unusual designs: one a platinum snake with its tail in its mouth and a small ruby for its visible eye; the other, a twist of gold braids fashioned to resemble a whip. Her third ring had been her mother's gold wedding band, studded with small sapphires. To make typing easier, she took the rings off carefully whenever she sat down at her desk and placed them in a Limoges ashtray located near her right hand. She put them on again whenever she left her small inner office to the rear of the suite of offices for the secretary of the university on the ground floor of Woodbridge Hall. Whenever she came to mind, Tony Celotto, that officer, pictured her sitting upright on her postural chair, just leaving for or returning from the ladies' room, her right hand worrying rings across the chubby knuckles of her fingers. Still, like his predecessor who had hired her, he valued her efficiency, her experience, her fierce loyalty and sense of responsibility to Yale. Those qualities balanced his distaste for her great weight, prodigious appetite, and dancing rings.

It was characteristic of Isabel that she let herself into Woodbridge Hall and then the Secretary's office in the late afternoon on the Friday after Thanksgiving, a university holiday. Without family, she hated holidays. She had left with the others after noon Wednesday so that

7

they would think she had somewhere to go. But she had gone home and remained there, alone. Now, after sulking through Thanksgiving, she needed to combat her loneliness. She needed something to do. She wanted also to make sure that she had overlooked no assignment when she had departed her office. Since the university was closed, she found no one else in the building. The top of her desk was clear, as she had left it, except for a package that surprised her. A card attached to the package carried a message that also surprised her: "For Isabel Doughton, Happy Thanksgiving," signed—so she thought—in a male hand: "A long-time admirer." But so far as she knew, she had no male admirers. Nor did she recognize the handwriting. Perhaps, she surmised, her benefactor—probably her boss—had a clerk sign the card.

She unwrapped the package carefully so as to preserve the red and yellow paper, which she intended to use again. It enclosed a silver-colored box of a dozen chocolate-covered cherries on a cardboard tray, that wonderful dark, French chocolate, from the confectioner, Georg Tremain, 12 rue de la Monde, Paris. Her favorite candies, she thought to herself, from someone who knew her tastes. She sat down and ate one. It was unusual, satisfying, hard on the outside, liquid inside, and followed by a pleasant, slight tingling on her tongue. She ate another. Same tingling and a taste of French cordial, all in all delicious. She ate a third. She folded the wrapping paper and put it in her tote along with the box containing the remaining candy. Making sure that both the office and the building were securely locked, she walked to her car parked on Wall Street and headed for home.

She had inherited from her father a small, Greek-revival house at the corner of East Rock Road and Livingston Street, about a mile away. Proceeding north along Whitney Avenue, she stopped at the traffic light on Canner Street and again at East Rock Road. While waiting for the lights to turn green, she ate another two pieces of candy. She consumed the rest of the candy while she changed clothes, putting on her father's best suit, a gray flannel chalk stripe, over her underclothes and one of his white shirts and red ties. Over his suit, she donned his academic gown, a Yale blue, and hood. Because of her bulk, she could no longer properly button the jacket, trousers or shirt, but she nevertheless cross-dressed when she felt especially good, as she had since finding the candy. It reminded her of the treats her father had lavished upon her as long as he had lived. It reminded her of him, still the center of her life.

Half an hour later, thirsty and standing at her stove waiting for water to boil for tea, Isabel began to feel weak. She turned down the kettle, walked slowly into her living room, and, loosening her robe and jacket, flopped onto her sofa. When the weakness persisted, she rose to go to the telephone but at first could barely move her legs. Quickly then she fell over, feeling totally paralyzed. She tried to shout for help but either had no voice or could not hear it. Lying on the floor, she became aware that she had trouble breathing. It became harder and harder to draw a breath, but she retained her terrified consciousness until, a few minutes later, she died. Her cleaning woman found the body when she came to work the following Tuesday. The woman screamed. Then, sobbing, but pulling herself together, she called the police.

"Shit," Stavros snapped, seeing the robed body on the floor, "What's this, an Old Blue Corpse?"

"But what a helluva way to die," the police medical examiner, Dr. Solomon Cohen, said. He and Detective Lieutenant Deno Stavros had just begun to examine the gruesome body. "She seems to have experienced total respiratory compromise, and from the look in her eyes and the distortion of her features, she seems to have been aware of what was happening. Poison, I expect, though I've no idea what kind. We'll have to see what an autopsy shows. Someone must have hated her."

"The maid said she was a hot-shot secretary at the university," Stavros replied. "Her father used to do something with theater—I remember him from when I was in high school. Must be dead now. She's got his clothes on. Trying to be a Yalie, I guess, like he was. He used to go 'round with a homburg, a stick and one of those coats with a velvet collar. Even at the Bowl, and he never missed a football game. Maybe some Harvard or Princeton type did her in. But not for love, I bet. Who's going to love someone that size?"

"You better call the Yale police," the M.E. said. "The university should know what's happened."

The two men had just arrived, summoned by a couple of junior detectives who had answered the dispatcher's emergency report of the maid's message. Now the detectives were standing around waiting for the police photographer to record the scene before the body was removed. Impatient with their indolence, Stavros snapped, "Okay you, Freeman, and you, Jensen, start searching the house for anything interesting, poison particularly. And check the trash. Check for fingerprints other than hers or the maid's. Get the lead out! We got a probable homicide here."

Stavros picked up the phone from a table next to the sofa and called the chief of the Yale police, Henry Fawcett. "Hi, Chief," he said, "we got a dead woman here dressed like she just got a Yale degree. Maid says she's Isabel Doughton, but we need an official identification, so you better get out here at Livingson and East Rock. Looks like poison." Hanging up, he went to find Jensen and Freeman who were exploring the kitchen.

They were an odd team, both products of unsubtle affirmative action. Peter Freeman, a black officer, had come up through the ranks from patrolman to detective. A flashy dresser, he played clarinet off duty in a local jazz combo. His superficial languor disguised his ambitious professionalism. Joan Jensen, his partner, blonde, lean, short and tough, had been recruited from the police force in Waterbury. She was still raw but eager.

"The deceased has prints on the kettle," Jensen told Stavros, "and on the tea cup, too. Maybe poison was in the tea."

"She didn't get to make tea, dummy," Stavros replied. "Look. The kettle is all burned out. Go see the maid, ask her if she turned off the stove. She's upstairs, resting."

A siren sounded just then, its pitch rising as the car approached. Stavros walked to the front door as Chief Fawcett braked to a stop and entered the house. "Jesus," Fawcett said when Stavros led him to the corpse, "What the hell happened to her? She looks as if someone scared her to death."

"Yeah, sure, to death," Stavros said. "Cohen will do an autopsy but she sure as hell knew she was dying, and that frightened her plenty."

They stood there in silence for a minute or two, each sizing up the other. Deno Stavros was half Greek, half Italian. His immigrant parents had founded "The Corinthian Pie," a popular pizza place on State Street north of the corner of Bradley. He had been a fireplug as a young man, a bruiser, catcher for Hillhouse High two years when they won the state championship. He joined the force after Pawtucket cut him from training camp. Stavros was a realist. He reckoned that if he got cut by Pawtucket, he would never make it big time. So he gave up games for the real world. Now in his middle years, he still looked muscular in spite of his expanding gut. And he was still a realist. He did not wholly trust Yale people, nor did he wholly trust blacks, and Fawcett was both Yale and black. But Stavros would try to get along with him. For all his tough talk, Stavros understood town-gown relations better than most city officials. Though he sometimes resented the university as an unfriendly sanctuary of wealth and privilege, he was privately proud that his sister worked in the treasurer's office and her son, his nephew, was beginning his freshman year. Still, he knew Yale officials played their cards close to their chests.

Now Stavros and Fawcett needed each other. Stavros needed Fawcett to interpret his methods to university faculty and administration. Fawcett needed Stavros to keep the city police under control and for real muscle if any became necessary. Fawcett was thinking about murder as they stood looking at the corpse. If someone had killed Isabel, it would be the first on his watch. He had no experience with murder. So he would have to lean on Stavros, whom he considered needlessly crude and bossy. He and Stavros had grown up in New Haven but in wholly separate communities. Younger than Stavros, Fawcett was just as athletic though his talent had blossomed at cornerback for Fairfield College. Whereas Stavros sported a paunch, Fawcett, still lean, had a pencil thin, gray mustache that accentuated the attractiveness of his graying hair. He meant to make women swoon. Each man, wary of the other, would nevertheless cooperate for a common purpose. Up to a point. Fawcett had no intention of informing Stavros about anything at Yale he didn't have to know in order to work the case. And Stavros, as always, suspected that all Yale officials preferred to keep the city in the dark.

Stavros spoke first: "Okay if we take her to the morgue?"

"Go ahead," Fawcett said. "Your people sweeping the house?"

"We've begun. My guess is fat stuff ate something poisoned. Who put the poison in it and why leads me to your Yalies and maybe the neighbors, most of them probably Yalies themselves. I need your help. What was her job? Any friends? Any enemies? Who should have missed her when she didn't come to work? Cohen guesses she's been dead since about last Friday. So how do you want to get started?"

"If you can hold my take on the Doughton woman until later, I'd like to report her death to President Stiles and to the secretary of the university, her boss, Tony Celotto, you know, Mama Celotto's son."

"I know Mama," Stavros said. "Everybody knows her Italian deli, best smells on Orange Street. Don't know the son but I've heard he's the first Italian to make it big at Yale."

"I guess," Fawcett said. "Isabel Doughton worked for him. She was his executive secretary. Ran that office like a Marine sergeant. She'd been at Yale forever. Practically an Old Blue like her father. Started in the president's office and moved to the secretary's before my memory begins. Knew her way around. Knew everyone in the fast lanes. But no lilac. Man, but did she ever throw her weight around! Thought her father was God and she was his only son. Always eating. And lived here alone. Hard to believe anyone but a parent loved her."

"A real doll, right? How about you go see the president," Stavros said. "Let me surprise Celotto. He should have been looking for her. Then I'll meet you for coffee at the Greek place on York Street and we can compare notes. About an hour from now."

"Okay," Fawcett said. "Only mind your manners. Tony Celotto is a gentleman and he's my boss, too."

"Trust me," Stavros said. "But I got to check on Jensen and Freeman first."

Walking to his car, Fawcett reflected that there had been a lot going on at Yale about which President Stiles would not want publicity. As Fawcett had only recently discovered himself, those goings on dated back at least until Labor Day and the beginning then of a search for a new president.

BOOK ONE

THE SEARCH

1.
LABOR DAY

The smoky light leaking through the shade of the east window signaled another typical New Haven day. "Color it gray," his children said of their town. Gray on Labor Day, an academic holiday, the last before term began. Jerry Walsh—Gerald Louis Walsh, professor of early American history at Yale University—tried to turn over and go back to sleep. Either he had awakened to the sound of Karen moving about the kitchen and listening to the Schubert string quintet, or Schubert's grand crescendos had awakened him. Jerry stretched all five feet seven inches of his mildly arthritic frame, leaned back with his head on his left palm and the back of his hand on his pillow, passed his right hand lightly over his thinning brown hair, and closed his eyes against the weak daylight. He had awakened an hour or so earlier, rolled over and brushed his wife's back. At once he had thought how it simplified life that the twins were away for the semester at Georgetown University in Washington, D.C. Because he dearly loved his wife. He loved her hands, a gardener's sure hands, loved the deft poems she wrote and often published in literary journals.

More immediately Jerry loved the sweetness of her body, its elegance and lithe strength. And so he reached for her, woke her slowly with a quiet kiss. Smiling she responded, shed her sleepiness and her gown, and joined him in their matinal romp. He had fallen back to sleep in their ensuing embrace, but Karen had left his side to tend to breakfast. Now wide awake, he smelt coffee curling up toward him.

With that aromatic reveille he realized the phone was ringing. Karen called that it was President Stiles and Jerry at once picked up.

"Morning, Jerry," came Arthur Stiles' familiar baritone. "Hope I didn't awaken you. I would like to see you as soon as possible today. Can you make it in an hour? The house, not the office. I'll have coffee here."

"I'll be there," Jerry replied, wondering what could be so urgent.

"What did Arthur want?" Karen called up the stairs.

"He said he needed to see me, but he didn't say why. May I have some juice and toast first? Thanks. I'll be down after I shave and shower."

Walking the half mile to the president's house, Jerry could not guess what Arthur Stiles had on his mind. It was unlike the King not to speak out. Jerry had known Arthur Stiles for some twenty-five years. As Professor Stiles years before he had taught the course on American colonial history that had provided the only intellectual spark in Jerry's freshman year. Arthur had presided over a seminar for juniors about Yale in the 18th century that had persuaded Jerry to try to make a career of history. Arthur had directed Jerry's senior essay on the common law in early Connecticut. Arthur had helped him expand that essay into his doctoral dissertation and then his first book. He was Arthur's friend and protégé. Indeed Arthur had pushed him along from rank to rank and endorsed him as his successor in the department when he became president. Arthur had even served as Jerry's best man when he married Karen, and Arthur and the beautiful Charlotte, his wife, a celebrated horticulturist, had treated Karen like a favorite niece. So whatever Arthur wanted, Jerry would almost certainly do.

President Stiles was a force at Yale and in the academy at large. A lean, relaxed and striking man only four inches short of seven feet tall, his head adorned with snow white hair, with a voice evocative of good breeding and easy self-confidence, Arthur E. Stiles was a descendent of Yale's late 18th century president, the Reverend Ezra Stiles. Like his forebears, Arthur Stiles graduated from Yale College where he was editor of the literary magazine and a Pundit—an undergraduate wit. After two years in his family's investment house in Boston, he had fled to Oxford for graduate study and then back to Yale where he established himself as an authority on the history of American education in the 17th and 18th centuries. Devoted to the university and deeply engaged in its affairs, Stiles made an enduring impression on his colleagues who were amused by his elegant wardrobe, delighted by his irreverent humor, and awed by his analytical mind. He was just about their unanimous choice for president when his predecessor died. The Fellows of the Yale Corporation agreed. They intended to appoint Arthur whatever the faculty thought, but they found faculty approval convenient and were pleased to let the faculty think its will prevailed.

The elegance, the manner, the height, the office, and "King Arthur" or "the King" entered common university parlance. As president, Arthur had the good sense to recognize that his crucial constituents were the faculty and students. He cultivated their interests with an unobtrusive skill that refurbished Yale's traditional distinction. The older faculty were, like Jerry, devoted to the King. He had supported their scholarship, recruited excellent students and rewarded good teaching. His priorities, however, did not include championship athletics or favoritism in admissions for alumni children, so he was less than popular with conventional alumni.

As Jerry approached 43 Hillhouse Avenue, the imposing Victorian structure that served as the president's residence, Arthur opened the door himself. "Greetings," he said. "Coffee's ready. We're going to use the living room." They walked together through the foyer and left into the parlor, then through the graceful living room with its cream walls and Yale-blue curtains from ceiling to floor. A John Marin seascape hung above the mantel. The King, an avid sailor, liked to keep the ocean near him. From the living room they could see into the dining room with its spectacular, dark green, linen wallpaper. Arthur motioned Jerry to an easy chair alongside of the fireplace and sat on the facing sofa. He poured coffee for them both from a handsome silver pot. "Let me get right to it," he said. "I've decided to resign as of next June 30. Now don't start arguing! Hear me out."

"At the risk of being rude," Jerry interrupted, "I have to say that you have been a marvelous president. No one in the country has been your equal."

"There are a lot of rich alumni who would disagree with that assessment," Arthur said, "and Yale needs their money. They don't like my policy on admissions to Yale College. Some of them resent my criticisms of the religious right, others dislike my support of affirmative action. And frankly, Jerry, it will have been twenty years next June and I'm tired. I've had to say no more often than I could say yes. That's made me some enemies even among the faculty you consider my allies. They want to take charge or at least to have a president who wants to go their way. Worse, the university is just about broke. We need more endowment for faculty salaries, for refurbishing our older buildings, for new laboratories and start-up facilities for the sciences. My temperament doesn't fit the spartan regime the Corporation demands until we have raised the funds for those purposes, which will take at least five to ten years. The Fellows also want to stress initiatives that will result in the university's making money through spin off arrangements with our scientists. They want Yale to follow the paths of M.I.T. and Stanford. But I do not, and I continue to believe the college above all should protect and promote humanistic studies. That's always been my style, and it seems out of fashion now."

"You know that I feel the same way," Jerry said.

"Yes, and I appreciate it," the King replied. "But not every one of your colleagues shares your view. So I'm counting on your diplomatic skills. I'll explain after you tell me whether you have any interest in becoming the next president."

"As you must surmise," Jerry said, "none at all. I've never wanted to be president or dean of any institution."

"As I thought," Arthur said wryly. "And as you know, you're not really fit for it. You'd be too much involved in details, too much the perfectionist, uncomfortable with power. You'd worry yourself to the grave. But I also have a more realistic question for you. How about serving as chair of a faculty committee to advise the Corporation about the presidential search? Prox Young, the senior Fellow, knows about my intentions and likes the idea of a faculty advisory committee. He is also a fan of yours. Indeed he wants to meet you for luncheon tomorrow if you're willing. And I want you to start thinking about who else should be involved so you can tell Prox."

"Yes, of course, if that's what you and he want," Jerry said. "But you must know that I'm devastated by the thought of your leaving. Yale will miss you, and the faculty will miss you. I'll be in a state of shock for days. And, Arthur, what will you do?"

"There is life after Yale, I'm sure. I've some ideas I'll tell you about some other time. Just now I must prepare myself to face the freshman convocation at 11 this morning. I'm going to talk about the importance of national service, and then I'll announce my plan to resign. Incidentally, Prox has reserved a private room for you two at Mory's at noon tomorrow."

"He's in character," Jerry said, "Mory's is as blue as he is. And your message is in character, too. For God, for country and all that. The freshmen will take your point before they graduate. I'll get out of your way now, but I have to say again how depressed I am at the thought of Yale without you."

Starting for his office, Jerry walked south on Hillhouse Avenue past the great houses lining it. Even though it was Labor Day the history department would be open so that faculty could prepare for registration Tuesday and classes Wednesday. He needed to use the duplicating machine to run off copies of the syllabus for his undergraduate course. The gray morning had become heavy, suiting his mood. On Grove Street he turned west to the corner of College Street, then crossed at the light and went through Hewitt Quadrangle where Beinecke Library, its translucent marble dulled by the weather, faced Woodbridge Hall. Continuing west on Wall Street, he approached the Hall of Graduate Studies and could see the windows of his second floor office. To his left bulked the Sterling Library with its heavy façades and great tower. Across the street from it stood the Law School, forming a canyon with the library and the Hall, all of them neo-Gothic in style, as was much of the campus. To Jerry, that architecture seemed ponderous especially on a gray day.

On impulse he turned into the Law School. With term about to begin, Professor Lilith Furman would surely be in her office, and a quiet chat with Lilith, a trusted colleague, would help to lift his flagging spirits. Lilith Furman had come to Yale from Harvard some ten years earlier as a professor, a former public defender in Boston, and a woman with a growing reputation in criminal law. She was also a refugee from a failed marriage to a Harvard chemist. She had since met and married Carter Jefferson, once Yale's assistant librarian for rare books, now head of the Morgan Library in New York. He and she lived on St. Ronan Terrace, just across the way from Karen and Jerry Walsh. With Carter in Manhattan several nights a week, Lilith and Karen, both accomplished cooks, often spent an evening comparing and testing recipes, most of them Italian as befit New Haven and, in Karen's view, a healthy diet. Jerry soon discovered that Lilith shared his interest in New England colonial law. She became his learned but informal adviser for his developing work on that subject. So homemade pasta and legal history, an odd couple, formed the basis for their friendship. Lilith towered over Jerry and Karen. Tall and stout but surprisingly agile, she had an alert manner, keen mind and quick sense of humor. She dressed to accentuate her size and wore large horn-rimmed spectacles for the same purpose. The total effect was at once formidable and pleasing.

Jerry entered Lilith's office as he knocked on her open door. Lilith, her eyes fixed of the screen of her laptop computer, muttered: "Yes." Then she looked up. "Oh, hi, Jerry. Good to see you. What brings you here? You look as if you lost your best pal."

"Just about," Jerry said. "The King is going to tell the convocation this morning that he'll resign next June. I'm under orders to chair a committee to advise the Fellows about the search for a successor. I hope you'll consent to serving on it. We need someone with your savvy and smarts."

"I bet you also need a woman," Lilith said.

"That, too," Jerry agreed, "and a representative of the law school and someone who is not an Old Blue to ruminate about a very Blue matter."

"You really want an old Crimson, A.B. and J.D., to advise about a Yale president? How generous! To be serious, I'm flattered. But I'm sorry the King is leaving. He's been a wonderful president, and he'll be hard to replace. It must be tough for you. You've been so close to him. I'm sure my good dean, Robert Whitney Humber himself, will be bucking for the throne. He's too self-righteous for me. Does that disqualify me?"

"We're advising the Fellows, not selecting the next president," Jerry replied, "and we shouldn't worry about candidates yet. After all, your neighbor and mine, Eugene Barnard, is bound to be on any list of wannabees. And Gene is a son of Yale as well as a popular lecturer. The undergraduates love him. He's my friend but I don't see that as disqualifying me."

"Then I'll gladly serve," Lilith said.

"That's a relief!" Jerry replied. "I'll let you get back to your work. I'll also tell Proxmire Young at luncheon tomorrow that you're full of zeal. I'll report his response before you're in Karen's kitchen again."

Betty Barnard, in her professional life Elizabeth Strafford, her maiden name, struggled to wake up in a bed that seemed strange and next to a man she needed a moment to recall. She had a ghastly hangover. There had been too many hangovers in the last two years, she told herself, too many early mornings in strange beds with strange men. But this morning her throbbing consciousness placed her companion. That bald head, she realized as she faced the day, belonged to Alan Goldstein, her partner of many years in the Bridgeport law firm of Harris, Strafford and Goldstein, tax specialists. Alan was a sweet man with a wife of his own. Usually Betty kept business and sex apart, but they had worked all Sunday and into the evening on a client's pending hearing with the IRS, dined late at a sleazy steak house near Milford, consumed too many stingers after dinner, and finished the day with some inebriated sex at a nearby motel. They had not had sex ever before and Betty regretted her lapse as much as she regretted her hangover. She would not let it happen again, she vowed to herself. Too complicated at the office.

Moving slowly to prevent any impact that might rattle her head, Betty crept out of bed and into the bathroom for a steamy shower. She dressed while Alan slept on, stepped out and into her Miata, and started for New Haven, for home, breakfast and a change of clothes. Her thoughts as she drove turned to her husband. She and Gene Barnard lived together at his insistence in order, he said, to protect his career from the taint of divorce. He had come to spurn her ever since she and her obstetrician had agreed in the third month of a pregnancy, her first and only, to abort a fetus with several missing chromosomes. The child would have been pitiful had it been born. But Gene wanted children and blamed Betty for not bearing any. He could also have blamed himself for refusing to adopt. As it was, he largely ignored Betty and buried himself in scholarship and in Yale affairs. A talented classicist and historian, he had published a best-selling account of the early Roman emperors, won a Pulitzer Prize, and had been working ever since on an interpretation of Tacitus which he could not seem to finish. He put more of himself into his teaching and his many committees, ladders as he saw them for an appointment to a senior administrative post. He probably failed to notice her absence the previous evening. She hoped to return to her client's tax case before he awakened. She was annoyed with herself less for falling into bed with Alan, dumb though that had been, than for deferring her intention to file for divorce from Gene.

B. (for Bernard) Proxmire Young looked the part he played in life. A big man in his mid-fifties, he worked out daily and enjoyed beating men twenty years his junior at squash. He also outsmarted most men of all ages in his management of his own and his clients' investments. Young had made millions of dollars. His large gifts to Yale, as he liked to boast, did not exceed the accumulated profits from his daily arbitrage in currencies. Those profits allowed him to endow four professorships, two in mathematics and two in economics, the fields he had chosen as an undergraduate for a combined major. As an undergraduate he also excelled as a fencer, a youthful master of the saber. That weapon resembled his usually concealed temperament. In his senior year he was elected to Phi Beta Kappa and to Loaf and Blade, a prestigious secret society with a membership from previous years that included Arthur Stiles. Selected as a Fellow of the Yale Corporation while in his early forties, Young had become Senior Fellow only recently. He reveled in the role.

Seated next to Arthur Stiles on the platform in Woolsey Hall, Young enjoyed every minute of the freshman convocation, particularly the silent but perceptible shock of the faculty members who were there when the King ended his remarks by announcing his intention to resign. As the procession of dignitaries then filed out, Young peeled off and walked over to the small office in Woodbridge Hall reserved for him over the weekend. Once settled at his desk, he turned to his notes about the budget. A few minutes later, there was a knock on his door. Surprised, he called out: "Who's there?"

"Hello, Mr. Young," Harry Grayson said confidently as he entered. "You may remember me. I'm one of this year's delegation to Loaf and Blade, so we met last spring. I just covered the convocation for the *Yale Daily News*, so I have to see you about who's going to be the next president."

"I know who you are, Harry," Young replied, "and I know your reputation as a hound for a scoop. But the search for the next president has yet to begin, so there's nothing to talk about except the significance of the search for Yale, if that subject interests you."

"There is something more important, sir, if I may contradict you," Harry said. "You're Senior Fellow and you should know right away about student opinion. I'm managing editor of the *News*, the *News* speaks for the students, so I'm here to promote their candidate, Professor Eugene Barnard. He's got everything Yale needs. Why, he's even a member of Loaf and Blade."

"Slow down, Harry," Young interrupted. "I know there is much to be said for Professor Barnard. He's an accomplished teacher and scholar, and be assured that I hold him in high regard. Indeed he's a friend. But your pitch for him is premature. More to the point, the *News* does not represent student interests. I doubt that medical or law students even read it."

"The *News* represents the undergraduates," Harry said, obviously perturbed. "They are the most important students. They'll be the big alumni contributors some day. They deserve a hearing."

"Harry," Young replied severely, "control your tongue! No one elected the *News* officers except Newsies themselves. If and when we conclude that undergraduates need a special hearing, we'll arrange a way to consult them. It won't be through the *News*. Meanwhile any undergraduate is free to meet with members of the Corporation search committee whose names and office hours I'll announce at a convenient time. I'll even give you a scoop about them if you behave yourself. Now I've work to do. Get along with you."

"Is the faculty going to have a committee?" Harry asked, pressing his chance.

"I'll let you know. Since you persist," Young said, "let me inform you that universities are institutions with a life of their own in which each generation of students shares but which no one generation of students should control. Decisions about the university's course through time belong to the Corporation. The Fellows are bound by oath to protect Yale's interests. The faculty, when consulted, may advise the Fellows. Obviously the faculty has a much longer experience of Yale than students do. But the Corporation will decide as long as I'm senior Fellow. Write your editorials. Leave governance to us."

"I'm leaving," Harry said, moving toward the door, "but don't underrate Eugene Barnard. He's a great teacher and he won a Pulitzer prize for his book on Rome. Believe me, he's the popular choice."

"You're pushing too hard. So that you'll have something to write about, I'll tell you that I'm asking Professor Walsh to head a faculty advisory committee on the search. But it's going to be a long haul. It will be at least several months before we have a full list. Now go."

"That's great," Harry said. "He and Professor Barnard are friends." With that, he left.

Harry Grayson's story, with his byline of course, covered the front page of Tuesday's *News*. It was accompanied by a glowing review of Arthur Stiles' contributions to Yale, along with flattering comments about the King by both Yale faculty and other university presidents. Almost the same material had filled the Monday evening TV news and appeared in Tuesday's *New York Times* and *New Haven Register*. All those accounts predicted there would be no decision about a successor for several months. All the accounts mentioned Eugene Barnard and Robert Humber as likely inside candidates.

ISABEL

Isabel was greedy—greedy for food, as her obsessive eating indicated; greedy for jewelry, as her extensive collection of expensive rings and brooches attested; greedy for love, the lack of which underlay all her greed. She had been unloved and felt unloved since the death of her father who had treated her as if she were royalty. For his part, he had been an ineffectual teacher of drama, an apostle of outmoded styles of acting. A Yale alumnus, B.A. and Ph.D., fixated on his college, he had struggled to remain as close to it physically as he was emotionally. He succeeded when a friendly classmate, temporarily provost, used his influence to arrange an appointment for John Doughton as a permanent lecturer in the Drama School. He never missed a home football game, never missed a Commencement and never ceased doting on Isabel, his only child. She became his only solace after his wife died in her thirties of polio. He expressed his adoration in regular treats of candies and cookies and occasional gifts of stunning jewelry.

After his death, only Isabel remained to spoil herself. Some of her former schoolmates lived nearby in New Haven, but they avoided her company. She knew she was unattractive. She even tried several times to lose weight. But invariably she surrendered to her appetites. On good days, when she had gone to see Yale play football or hockey while pretending to accompany her father, or when she stuffed herself with something especially tasty, she celebrated by wearing her father's clothes, sometimes also his cap and gown. Then she felt as if he were with her, as if he were stroking her, as if she were loving him in return, and she played with herself. Because that habit made her feel at once excited and guilty, she worried about it, but she never gave it up.

So, too, dipping into her father's modest estate, she slated her greed whenever she could afford to. Greed particularly consumed her when she was alone at home for a few days. Consequently weekends were hard for her. That Labor Day evening, a platter of chocolate brownies at her side, Isabel sat, filled with self- pity, in the porch off the south wall of her living room. She had talked to no one since her office closed the previous Friday. Now out of sorts, she yearned to satisfy her craving for the emerald brooch advertised by Cartier on the third page of the first section of the morning *Times*. Emeralds on platinum arranged like a sprig of leaves dotted with diamond rain. Six figures and worth it but beyond the limits of her purse.

Isabel was also a snoop. Since she had no friends, snooping, in a sick way, satisfied some of her need for intimacy. She constantly spied on her next-door neighbors who had discovered her when, at a Columbus Day street party, she carelessly remarked about the color of the new pajamas of the man of the house. Thereafter those neighbors kept down the shades in the rooms facing Isabel's home. She snooped on her frequent nightly strolls along College Woods, a western section of East Rock Park, which lay just across the street from her residence. Hidden by the dark shadows there, she used powerful binoculars to peer into any unguarded windows of the dwellings on Livingston Street. Now and then she saw things that no one was intended to see.

On Sunday night, the previous night, with insomnia gripping her, she had set out just before midnight. On the northeast window of the second floor of the house halfway down the block, the drawn curtains, blown apart by an intermittent east wind, revealed just enough for her to observe Robert Humber, the proud dean of the Law School, dressed in a bra and panties with a woman in a police uniform beating him with a thin cane. Isabel felt a shudder of excitement. Another transvestite! And surely, as she was, consumed with guilt as well as arousal. So Humber would be vulnerable, and at her convenience, she could exploit his vulnerability.

Now, on Monday, she had heard the evening news about President Stiles' pending resignation. Humber would covet Stiles' office. That gave her the perfect opportunity to strike. Reaching for a pencil and pad, she drafted a note:

> *You were seen in unusual clothing taking a beating from a cooperative woman. Your wife? Is that how you get it off? Would you like me to report the episode to the Yale Daily News? Harry Grayson would relish the scoop. Think about it, and I'll be in touch.*
> *Your observant Snoopy*

That would just about do it, Isabel concluded. On Tuesday, when she reached her office, she would enter the note she had drafted on the word processor of her desktop computer, print it out and save it on the hard disk. Her secret access code protected her files there. And a printout, unlike a typed or handwritten document, could not be traced. She would let Robert Humber sweat for a while. Then she would demand payment. He should be good for five figures, perhaps half the cost of the brooch. She would collect it in installments to give him time to raise the money, and time for his ambitions to motivate him to pay. Isabel was pleased with herself. When she had finished with Humber, she would find others to satisfy the rest of her needs.

2.
LUNCHEONS

Under ordinary circumstances Prox Young would have booked his favorite table at Mory's for his luncheon with Jerry Walsh the Tuesday after Labor Day. He liked to sit at table 30, a table for two just at the side door to the bar and only a step or two from table 31 where the Wiffenpoofs sat when they gathered to sing on Monday evenings. But he did not want to be overheard, so he booked a small private room behind the rear stairs to the second floor. Mory's was a private club but any Yale undergraduate could join if he or she was willing to pay the inexpensive dues, and any could purchase a life membership, though relatively few did. Over the years some Yale faculty who came to the university from elsewhere had also been allowed to join. So Mory's, renowned in song for the Wiffenpoofs, while nominally private, had a quintessentially Yale flavor. On a normal weekday in term time, like the Tuesday on which Prox awaited Jerry, there arrived for luncheon several deans, a few librarians, three or four alumni who lived in the area, and a goodly number of faculty. Much Yale business was unofficially transacted at Mory's in spite of the unchanging menu, the excessively fatty and salty cuisine, and the rather cramped space. Both Proxmire Young and Jerry Walsh loved the place.

Jerry always ate the same luncheon, number three on the menu, a bowl of soup, half a club sandwich and a cup of coffee. He expected to order just that when he walked through the foyer and main dining rooms to the back stairs, passing on the walls framed photographs of Yale varsity teams or of their captains, including one of him in hockey garb. He had been a small but quick and smart forward until in his senior year an Army defense man threw a wicked cross-check at him, knocked him against the boards, and broke his right thigh bone. Thereafter Jerry gave up contact sports.

Jerry looked around as he proceeded, taking in the familiar décor—wainscoting on the walls some four feet high; above the wainscoting textured grass wallpaper, an amber-stained beige; and, set close to each other, oak trestle tables marked by the carved initials of generations of Yale students. Pending from the ceiling, huge inverted lanterns cast a yellow light. Above the tables, fastened to the dark beams, were shellacked oars of Yale crews victorious over Harvard in the annual four-mile race. The oars carried a message. One read: "Yale vs. Harvard--New London--June 19-1914--Time 21-16--J.A. Appleton Stroke." A great nephew of Appleton had enrolled in Jerry's lecture course a decade ago, and Prox Young, as it happened, managed the investments of that nephew's sister. Especially in the ambience of Mory's, Yale remained in some ways an institution of cousins, uncles and their friends, but Yale was changing and would change faster when Arthur Stiles left.

Prox Young, sipping a glass of white wine, motioned to a chair next to him as Jerry reached their private room: "Drink? Glad you could make it. I'm counting on you to give me a big helping hand."

"No thanks to the drink," Jerry said. "I'm flattered to be asked to help, and I know how important it is to find the right person to succeed Arthur."

"Then you must be thinking about who should join you on the advisory committee," Prox said. "I'd like to review the names with you. But here's the waiter. Luncheon is on me. I'm having the number three on whole wheat toast, coffee after the meal"

"The same," Jerry said, and the waiter departed.

"You must know," Prox then continued, "how heavy a burden is the president's collar, both physically and metaphorically."

"Yes," Jerry replied, "of course I've seen the King wearing it, though I've never actually picked it up."

"Metaphor aside, it's quite something," Prox said. "It was a gift to Yale, I've forgotten from whom, specifically for the sole use of the president on official occasions like yesterday's convocation or commencements, events like those. It consists of a chain of 25 carat gold pieces, very thin, strung on links of gold filigree. An eye on the top of the chain hooks into a loop on the back of the president's special gown, the one he wears for academic processions. Attached to the chain's bottom is a heavy gold shield, a heraldic device that hangs against his breastbone. There's a large blue sapphire in the center of the shield, Yale blue, of course. It's surrounded by diamonds, cut stones, not chips. Engraved on the shield is 'Lux et Veritas.' The whole thing's worth a mint and weighs a ton. But I digress! We're concerned about who's going to wear it."

The waiter returned with their meals and while they ate they discussed the uncertain prospects of the football team. Emptying his coffee cup, Prox returned to their business: "I'd like to tell you the qualifications that seem to me essential for the next president. Please understand that I have the highest regard for the King. He's been exactly the right man for the last twenty years. But I agree with him that twenty is enough. Yale now needs a different kind of president, someone less controversial, an inside man who does not try to address public issues. Arthur is wonderfully civilized, and he's the ultimate gentleman. He has beguiled the undergraduates and spoiled the faculty. But now is the time to cultivate the alumni, to build up the endowment, to refurbish the campus and to improve the business management of the university. We should also do more with engineering and the sciences that inform the dynamic technologies. There's money to be made that way. We have to get on the stick in order to survive. Yale needs a business-minded consolidator as president, a practical man, not a philosopher or aspirant secretary of state."

"The King," Jerry said, more abruptly than he had meant to, "has put Yale in the public eye, strengthened the faculty and student body, lifted Yale's national standing. We'll be lucky to find another president of his caliber. So with respect, your assessment doesn't appeal to me, though I agree that the alumni mood deserves attention."

"You don't have to agree. You have only to report my view to your committee. That view, I predict, will come to prevail as you go about your assignment. I don't want a faculty committee to act as a rubber stamp for me. I want a dialogue, and I believe even you, a personal friend of Arthur's, as I am, will in the end accept my analysis."

"That's fair enough," Jerry replied. "Shall we turn to the membership of the committee?" Prox nodded and Jerry continued: "The members must command the respect of the faculty. So they have to have a record of creative scholarship and involvement in university affairs. As a group, they should also be representative of the major parts of Yale, not just the college, though I personally consider the college the paramount part. As a historian, I represent the humanities. Roger Gordon in psychology, a gifted teacher and a scholar with impressive publications on the pitfalls of intelligence testing, qualifies to represent the social sciences. Charlie Lee has an enviable international standing in physics, and he happens also to be of Chinese descent, therefore by federal guidelines a minority professor, though his personal brilliance and cheerful manner commend him regardless of race. We need a dean, and I rate Noah Montefiore at the top. Under his guidance the Medical School has become a major center for biological research, so he adds to the scientific input. All of them are graduates of Yale College except for Gordon who received his Ph.D. here. All are my friends, I admit, but I control none of them.

"I'd add two others to the committee," Jerry continued. "Professor Lilith Furman of the Law School, a specialist in criminal law, is the quickest study I have ever known, male or female. She was Harvard all the way, which will bring an outsider's view to the selection process. And we need a secretary. For that job the ideal person seems to me to be Tony Celotto, Yale through and through, and your brother in Loaf and Blade. I should add that I have ruled out Gene Barnard and Robert Humber because they are obviously candidates for the presidency, and ruled out, too, the admirable former provost, Richard Mason, a close friend who has consistently declined offers to become president of other institutions. He insists he wants no more administrative work. But we should consult him. He has knowledge of Yale unmatched by anyone but the King, and he is an expert on the economics of higher education. And that's it."

"Good list," Prox said after a moment of reflection. "I agree about consulting Mason, but whatever his personal preferences, he's too close to the King to be on my list of faculty possibles. So, of course, are you, but you assure me you don't want the job. Are all of Arthur's pals afraid to follow him? I also agree about leaving out Barnard and Humber. Gene is high on my private list, maybe at the top, but I've no personal enthusiasm for Humber. He's too vain and ambitious for me, and too inflexible in his public views. Why, he'd dispense with the Corporation if he were president and had the chance."

"You're too hard on Bob," Jerry interrupted. "He's a big talent whose virtues are hidden until you get to know him."

"Okay for now," Prox said. "I realize others will want Humber, and I'll hear them out but I'll take a lot of convincing. I don't know Roger Gordon or your Law School woman, but they sound right. It falls to me, speaking for the Fellows, to announce the committee, which I'll do by press release later this afternoon."

"That's great," Jerry said. "What about the Corporation? Are you going to have a committee of your own?"

"Yes," Prox replied. "I have to review the last minutes with Tony Celotto before I announce the membership. You'll know by nightfall. Incidentally, I consider Tony as a possible but unlikely candidate. Does that bother you?"

"No," Jerry said. "I know you Loaf and Blade types scratch each other's back, but Tony is too much a long shot to be excluded, and Gene is Loaf and Blade, too. Tony has two incomparable assets. He keeps his mouth shut, and he has a dandy executive secretary who will type and file our minutes for him. She's all blue and completely reliable."

"You mean the fatty in his office? I'll take your word for it."

"Her name is Isabel Doughton. You're sure to see something of her. She likes to be called Miss Doughton. You probably knew her father, a sort of sad man in the Drama faculty."

"John Doughton?" Prox asked rhetorically. "He was a Jack Spratt. How did he get a two-ton daughter?" Rising, he waited for Jerry to depart and followed him out.

Leaving Prox in front of the Hall of Graduate Studies, Jerry felt that the luncheon had been a success. He could work with Proxmire Young, he thought, because Young seemed straightforward. So long as they could talk candidly, as they had at lunch, they would get along.

On Wooster Street in New Haven, in the old Italian district of the city, somewhat toward the northeast end of the street, stands Pepe's, a pizza parlor which claims to have invented the pizza—the cheese pie—for which it is justly famous. In a booth in the back, a pitcher of beer between them, Tony Celotto and Lilith Furman were sharing a large pizza with toppings of mushrooms, peppers, bacon and Italian sausage. Both big eaters, both had cast iron digestions. Tony had invited Lilith for a private lunch after Jerry Walsh, early that Tuesday morning, had called him to discuss membership on the faculty committee to advise the Corporation. Tony and Lilith enjoyed all good food, Tony because his mother had brought him up on it, Lilith because she was a gourmet, leaning toward gourmand.

"Jerry is with Proxmire Young talking shop," Tony said, pouring more beer for them both. "I have to see Young after lunch to go over the minutes of the Fellows' meeting on their selection committee. You know Prox is a control freak. He speaks softly but, if I may mix my metaphors, stacks the deck to have his way. He'll announce his committee today so you might as well know about it now. Almost entirely men he can manipulate. Peter Manning, the Episcopal Bishop of Connecticut, is one of those, and so is Governor Billy Murphy. He's an Irish-American pharmacist who built up a chain of drug stores with a large loan from Young's firm to help him expand, and he's as solid a Republican as Prox himself. Manning is vain and unctuous, Murphy is affable and conventional, and neither knows much about Yale, so they'll follow Prox's lead. That gives Prox a majority. The other two have the virtue of independence. Prox had to include an alumni Fellow, one of those elected for seven-year terms, and the others imposed Charley Dray on him. You may know Dray. He's a local lawyer, a decent guy but too close to Bob Humber to be neutral in the search. And for genuine independence there's Sis Overman. Prox didn't want a woman but the other Fellows insisted. Good thing, too."

"I don't know any of them but Senator Overman whom I've met a few times," Lilith said. "Isn't her first name Barbara? And wasn't she appointed to the Senate to fill the unexpired term of her brother? And isn't she a sort of populist Democrat with roots in Iowa's good soil?"

"That's our Sis, who's also a Yale law product. Of course she's not any longer in office. She practices law in Washington in her hot shot firm, all women partners, Overman, Kelly and Krause. She and Prox argue about something at every meeting of the Corporation."

"She can't be a Humber fan."

"Oh, no," Tony said. "She's left of the political center and he's at the far right."

Lilith selected another piece of pizza, which dripped grease onto her paper plate. "He's a successful dean, you know," she said, wiping her chin. "Raises a lot of money. Still teaches a popular antitrust course. Pompous, yes, a former Rhodes scholar who's never recovered. Wears those bespoke three-piece suits, and he's a name-dropper, federal judges, senators, cabinet ministers, the works. But he's got the smarts, does a lot of consulting in Washington, mostly conservative think tanks, and cultivates the law school alumni who love him. The faculty likes the amenities he provides and their generous salaries."

"Still, why does he hang out with so many political dinosaurs?"

"He really believes in the so-called free market," Lilith replied. "That's why he's so serious about antitrust law. While he was getting close to the Reagan administration he met all those right-to-life Republicans and bought into their party line, including the religious stuff, school prayer and the rest of it. So he and Arthur Stiles have at each other through the press. They try hard never to meet."

"It speaks well for the King that he keeps Humber as a dean," Tony said. "You're right that Humber is polite. He cultivates my executive secretary who rarely has admirers. Gives her chocolates. She thinks he's wonderful."

"She doesn't need chocolates, if you mean Isabel Doughton. Too much of Isabel as it is."

"Go easy on her," Tony said. "I trust her and rely on her. And she kindly overrates me. She told me this morning that I ought to be the next president. That's unrealistic, I know, but I enjoy the fantasy."

"Really?" Lilith asked. "Jerry, of course, runs away from the idea. He'd be surprised to hear about your daydreams."

"Yale has been very good to me," Tony said. "Charlotte Stiles, one of my mother's customers, told her how to get me a tuition scholarship to Choate, and helped me find a job as a stack rat in the library to earn the money for an old VW bug so that I could commute during my last two years in secondary school. Then Choate introduced me to the glories of English letters, far from the surroundings of my Italian boyhood, and pushed me toward a scholarship at Yale. I majored in English—what a great department—and went on to earn the M.A. But I didn't have it for college teaching, so I was glad to accept an offer to become a baby dean of undergraduates. Then Arthur Stiles made me assistant to the secretary of the university and a few years later promoted me. I know I've been good at town-gown relations. Hell, I began reconciling Italians and their black classmates when I was still in junior high school. I know I get along with both the Fellows and the faculty. I honestly believe I could handle the presidency, and I'd sure like to try. But I'm even more sure that Yale will choose a scholar, as it should, and I'll bet you even money on Gene Barnard against the field."

"I like Gene, too," Lilith said. "He's somewhat slippery, though. I'm not certain I really trust him. We have a long way to go but I agree that he and Humber are now leading the pack. As for you, Tony, thanks for being so honest with me. You deserve every break you have had, and who knows what will emerge from a search that's yet to begin?"

"Yes, we'll see, but I don't expect to figure much in the process except as secretary to the Fellows' committee. Even in that role, about all I'll do is take notes that Isabel will transcribe. She'd be a weighty candidate, wouldn't she?"

"She considers herself a genuine Old Blue," Lilith replied, "and she wants you to get the job so you can appoint her dean of the Drama School. That way she can memorialize her father about whom she constantly talks."

"Yeah, but don't believe everything she says," Tony replied. "Prox is about to show up in my office, so I'll ask for the check and get going or he'll have to spend the afternoon with Isabel."

"This is Dutch," Lilith said, finishing the last of the pizza, handing Tony a ten dollar bill, and rising to depart.

Karen Walsh had luncheon that Tuesday with her friend and near neighbor on St. Ronan Terrace, Sylvia Wheatley, a skillful painter of children's portraits whose late husband had been a historian of medieval England, a colleague of Jerry's. They were seated in Karen's spacious kitchen, a sunny room with a brick tiled floor, warm yellow walls and avocado green window curtains depicting nursery stories. Karen had bought the curtains when the Walsh twins were only four, but she could not bring herself to replace them for they carried memories of so many happy times with Mark and Mary. The two women sat at the long table facing west and catching some of the early afternoon sun. They had finished their grilled cheese sandwiches and were addressing a fresh fruit cup and the rest of their iced coffee.

"You know," Sylvia said, "there are all kinds of rumors that Gene Barnard is going to be the next Yale president. At Mama Celotto's grocery an hour ago I heard almost nothing else."

"Your curiosity will kill you some day," Karen said. "Why, the search has not begun!"

"I admit I'm curious but I'm also fond of Gene, and he wants the presidency so much. I feel sorry for him. He and Betty have been at odds since she lost that baby, and he gets the worst of it while Betty gets around."

"Betty would tell you a different story if you asked her," Karen suggested. "How do you know so much about Gene?"

"He asked me to lunch the other day when we happened to leave our houses at the same time. I almost backed into his car. He's lonesome. Does him good to talk to an old friend and neighbor."

"Not too often," Karen said, "or the whole neighborhood will be talking."

"I'm not involved with Gene," Sylvia replied. "I doubt he'll ever get the presidency. After all, what would he do for a first lady? Betty goes off on her own all the time. Gossip says she's sleeping around. If so, that will kill his chances."

"Don't believe gossip in this part of town," Karen said. "Professors love to gossip and so do their wives. The Yale community is made to sound as bad as Peyton Place. Gene is a friend of ours and so is Betty, though we've seen too little of her lately. She's a busy lawyer, so gossip converts her professional absences into amorous encounters. I agree that Betty wouldn't want to give Yale affairs the kind of devotion Charlotte Stiles has. But neither would you or I. Faculty wives have careers of their own now. They can't be expected to put themselves at their husband's disposal the way their mother's generation did. I think Gene would make a good president with or without Betty, maybe better for her without."

"You and I are still pretty conventional women," Sylvia said. "It's always been proper for faculty wives to paint, as I do, or to write poetry, as you do, though I suppose you threaten the men by having so much of yours published. Your daughter's generation will expect the faculty, or a large part of it, to be women, and the president to be a woman, too."

"And rightly so," Karen replied.

On her bedside table Tuesday morning Betty Barnard, when she awakened, found a note from Gene asking her, if she possibly could, to join him for luncheon at the New Haven Lawn Club. Avid for racquet games, they had been members for a decade or more, with Gene more active than she was. The note was civil. Betty decided somewhat reluctantly that a civil conversation with Gene might do both of them good. But would he behave?

As she drove into the parking lot just before one o'clock and looked for an empty space, Betty saw Gene in his tennis whites bidding goodbye to a man she could not identify who was leaving through the front entrance. Gene met her as she parked. "Thanks for coming," he said. "Why don't you go in and find us a quiet table, and order a whiskey for yourself and an Elm City beer for me?"

"Done," Betty replied. She walked in the front door of the neo-colonial building, turned right and right again to the stairway to the lower level. There the luncheon room faced the tennis courts with changing rooms off the corridor leading to it. An empty table stood just beyond the entrance to the room with the tables around it also empty. Members who were eating had seated themselves on the terrace outside where they could watch the tennis underway strenuously on every court. Betty glanced at the players, most of them women, and sat down. When a waitress appeared she ordered drinks, two iced teas, a turkey sandwich for Gene and a chef's salad for her. She was sipping her Scotch—J&B as usual—when Gene arrived, his hair still damp, his tan chinos beautifully pressed, his sport shirt showing its predictable Lacoste alligator. Still the perfect preppie, Betty thought to herself, but how I once adored him!

"You look pleased," she said aloud. "Something good happen?"

"I beat the new assistant squash coach in two sets. You saw him in the parking lot on his way back to the gym. How did you know I wanted a turkey sandwich?"

"Have you forgotten that we've been married for a long time? This isn't our first lunch together. Do you ever order anything else?"

"Not often," Gene said, "but thanks for remembering. Look, I don't want to argue. I've been eager to have a heart-to-heart with you, okay?"

"That would be refreshing," Betty said "and pleasant, too. What's in your heart?" Gene, she reflected, could still be charming when he tried.

"I suppose you think only blackness," Gene said, "and I don't entirely blame you. I've been rotten, and I know it. But let's let bygones be bygones, and let's be honest with each other. The loss of the baby killed my desire, my love if you like. You know that. But I've been thinking. You can have a divorce if you want one. After all, you know the legal ropes. But I would contest one. Or we can try to get along for six months and see whether any old feelings return. I've had enough of living in an armed camp. It's exhausting. I suggest we try reconciliation and give up recrimination. How about it?"

"I'm not so sure that's enough for me," Betty replied. "Love used to be a beacon in my life. I don't really want to live without it, or without sex, either, and I'm not ready to start sleeping with you again."

"I'm aware of all that," Gene said, sourly. "I hear about your escapades, and I would expect you to give them up. I've not mentioned them before because I felt guilty about the way I was treating you. Now I propose a friendly arrangement with the chance, admittedly an outside chance, of something more developing. It once did. But can I count on you to keep up appearances? I want people to stop talking about us."

"I'll have to think about it," Betty said, finishing her salad and beckoning the waitress who came over to the table. "More iced tea, please," Betty said, "and some extra lemon."

"Make that two," Gene added, continuing after the tea was served. "You sound rather cool. I'm not suggesting a permanent arrangement, just a six-month trial in good faith. And I'd expect you to go easy on the booze."

"I'm not sure in my own mind why I haven't long since filed for divorce," Betty said. "Maybe I was punishing myself for not wanting children. Maybe I was punishing you for your attitude. I'm not ready to tie my hands for six months, but I'll give it a shot on a day-by-day basis. As for the drinking, that's my business. I've never embarrassed you in public, and I don't intend to. So stop being so damn pontifical."

"I need six months," Gene said. "I don't ask for more. Yale is appointing a new president and I want the job. It's mine. I have just the right qualifications so long as you and I appear a loving couple. Then if you want out, I promise not to object."

"Gene, you bastard!" Betty spit out the words. "I should have suspected that you had an ulterior motive for turning on the charm. God knows I don't want to preside in 43 Hillhouse. I'm no Charlotte

Stiles, much though I admire her. And I couldn't devote myself to you or to Yale now that I know what motivates you. To hell with you and your reconciliation."

"Not so fast," Gene said, "and lower your voice! You wouldn't want your partnership to go on the rocks, would you? It just might if I tell Hanna Goldstein about you and Alan."

Betty paled. "How did you know about that?" she asked. "Damn you, you're spying on me!" Raising one eyebrow, Gene nodded. "What an outrageous thing to do," Betty snapped. "It would destroy Hanna if she found out, and that would ruin Alan. He loves her. He was just drunk, and so, I admit, was I."

"He should have thought about Hanna before he hopped into bed," Gene replied. "And you had better think about her now. Because I mean business. I'll spill the beans unless you play our game my way. It's only for six months."

"That's blackmail!" Betty said. Then she ruminated for a moment. "No guarantees, but okay day-by-day as long as you mind your manners and control your tongue. And I may change my mind any day. I'm doing this for Alan and Hanna, not for you, so I want your notarized promise, I'll arrange for it, that you'll tell them nothing and in six months give me an uncontested divorce. Then as far as I'm concerned you're history. Those are my terms or I'll file for divorce now."

"Those conditions are acceptable to me, counselor," Gene said. "You'll be surprised to discover how very nice I can be."

"Nothing you do will surprise me ever again," Betty said, standing up from the table. "I hope those bulldogs on the Corporation realize how nasty you are. I'll probably see you tonight but I don't look forward to it."

"Smile when you say that," Gene said, grinning. "You may be talking to the next president of Yale."

ISABEL

Isabel had luncheon alone, quickly, at her desk. She had carried to work a diet Coke and some cottage cheese with late season raspberries. That menu struck her as slimming. But as she finished the Coke, she began thinking about what she had planned for Robert Humber, and in her excitement she reached into the bottom drawer of her desk and extracted from the goodies stored there two large chocolate chip cookies. She had arrived at work early enough to type her note to Humber and save it on her computer. Now she retrieved and printed it. But better not mail it from a New Haven post box, she decided. Why not mislead him? She recalled her summers with her father in a house he rented on the shore in Stony Creek. Mail it from there, his voice seemed to tell her.

She walked to her car, parked conveniently just yards from her office, and drove to the ramp to Interstate 95, across the Quinnipiac bridge, as usual heavy with traffic, and on east to Stony Creek where she mailed the note at the post box nearest her childhood residence. On the way back, to celebrate, she drove through a Dairy Queen to pick up a chocolate shake which she consumed before she reached the campus again. It had been just the right lunch hour—really ninety minutes—she reflected. Now to prepare Tony Celotto's spacious office for his afternoon meeting with Proxmire Young. She didn't need to be a fly on the wall, she assured herself. She had typed the minutes of the last Corporation meeting, and Tony had told her she would be typing the future minutes of both the Fellows' search

44

committee and the faculty committee advising it. The information in those minutes, she knew, might be worth more to her than anything she could see through her neighbors' windows.

3.

BEGINNINGS

In announcing President Stiles' resignation, Proxmire Young had described him as the greatest university president of his time, a true son of Yale, an outstanding American whose alma mater, forever in his debt, would miss his imaginative leadership. Young had also announced a worldwide search for a successor. But among the Yale faculty the assumption prevailed that one of their own would be the next president. Yale students, equally parochial, agreed. Gossip on Wednesday within both groups bandied about the same names, Barnard and Humber, more than any others, but also Sis Overman who had support among the few women professors; Tony Celotto, whose office and affability seemed sufficient credentials to many undergraduates; and two Yale alumni, Dean Jonathan Rose of the Columbia Law School and Vice President George Bush.

That evening Gene watched television in the upstairs room where Jerry and Karen Walsh kept their set. On the excuse of picking up some fresh tomatoes Karen had offered him, he had dropped by just in time for the news. He had hoped that Jerry would have some inside information to report. Indeed he would have settled for some juicy gossip. But Jerry, who knew only what was in the public domain, was disinclined even to discuss the news. Once the TV was off and they were all having a drink, Gene, his curiosity overflowing, asked Jerry how he thought the search would come out. "I'm naturally interested," Gene said, "and I suppose that you and the King must have thrashed it all out."

"On the contrary," Jerry replied. "Except for asking me whether I would be willing to chair the faculty committee, the King said nothing about the search and I doubt he will, especially to me. I'm sure he'll bend over backwards to avoid influencing the decision. That's his way. I'll tell you this, though; I'm going to miss him. It's hard for me to imagine anyone else as president."

"I'll miss him, too," Gene said, "but it's time. Yale needs to move ahead in new directions."

"Maybe so, maybe not," Jerry said. "I'd rather not talk about it at least until after the committee has decided. Once we get organized, every faculty member who wants to will have a chance to express his views about Yale and about candidates. I'm sure you will be the choice of many of them, Gene, but it would not do for me to give a friend an inside track. So let's wait."

"I'm less sure than you seem to be," Gene replied. "Of course I want to be considered. It's flattering to hear my name mentioned so often. But others are surely more experienced in administration, Bob Humber, for example. And classics seems an old fashioned place to look for a college president."

"More anon," Jerry said, determined to drop the topic. "Look, how about you stay for supper? Channel Three is carrying the Red Sox-Yankees game later and I've some good, dark beer."

"Thanks, but not tonight. Betty told me at lunch she'd see me at home. I'm late now." With that Gene left, pleased that he had had a natural chance to imply, bending the truth only slightly, that he and Betty were cozy.

Jerry mused about their conversation. He liked Gene and enjoyed his company, but if Gene pressed him about the search, their friendship would be strained. More important, Gene seemed to him too eager. That made him vulnerable. Humber was probably just as anxious. When people were that intense they were prone to make mistakes. He hoped he and his committee could stay relaxed and avoid controversy. He had selected the members partly with that purpose in mind.

"Penny for your thoughts," Karen said.

"I'm worried about Gene. He's pressing too hard."

"I agree," Karen said. "What's more he's being indiscreet. He asked Sylvia Wheatley to lunch last week, and according to Janet Sterne, who played tennis at the Lawn Club today, he and Betty had a brawl while lunching there. He'd better practice more self-control."

Except for Charlie Lee, who practically lived in his lab, the members of Jerry Walsh's committee disliked spending any part of a Saturday on campus. But the first week of registration and classes made it impossible to find any other common time, so they had agreed to Jerry's plea for a short session just to get started. They had known each other for years. Indeed, again except for Lee, a confirmed bachelor, they were all often together at social as well as academic functions. Lee, a decade older than the others, had a different set of personal friends. With his short white hair and face full of deep wrinkles, he looked the elder statesman he was. So in a different way did Noah Montefiore who believed that it behooved him as a dean to appear solemn. To that end he had grown a pronounced goatee, conveniently gray. His wife thought the whiskers made him look like a wimp, but Noah thought he looked like Louis Pasteur, which he considered a triumph.

Banter filled the room until Jerry called for order. "Tony can't be here today," he said, "so I'll keep the minutes. Let's get started." They all then quickly agreed to post special office hours for colleagues or students who wanted to see them about the search. Jerry would have ended the meeting at that point had not Robert Gordon predicted that few students would actually appear at the scheduled hours. Roger had a reputation as an expert on undergraduate psychology, so the others gave weight to his comment.

"Why not?" asked Noah Montefiore. "They seem to want a voice in the selection."

"The Newsies say they do," Roger replied, "but most undergraduates are curious but without firm convictions about candidates. They don't know what the presidency entails. They know only which teachers they like and whom they trust. That's why they think of Tony as well as Gene Barnard. Humber is out of sight for the undergraduates but they know about him from the press. And don't get me wrong. I'm all for scheduling the special office hours. If no one shows up, I can use them to catch up on correspondence."

"We all know Gene's a charter member of the King's club of classroom demagogues," Lilith said, "but he's better than that."

"I agree," Roger said, "but that kid Harry Grayson is acting like Gene's campaign manager. Gene should draw and quarter him."

"I'm reasonably sure it won't come to that," Jerry said. "After all, Gene's a bona fide candidate who needs no manager. He's a splendid scholar, too, so let's not make fun of him in our committee meetings. Fun at cocktail parties will be okay. In that environment he can take care of himself. Any acceptable candidate will have to take care of himself."

"Or herself," Lilith added.

"To be serious now," Charlie Lee said quietly, " I know everybody wants to go home, but one or two things need to be mentioned. Yale has called for a global search, right? No one will believe it was worldwide if we select a member of this committee. So if anyone here wants the job, better he leaves now." He grinned. "Or she," he said. Lilith laughed, as he had hoped she would.

"No one of us does, I think," Jerry said. "In my opinion no one of us is qualified except perhaps Noah. Roger is hopeless as an administrator, as he admits. Lilith might be wonderful but she's without experience. Charlie is too old, though he's a more distinguished scholar than anyone we'll find. And I want no part of any administrative post. So no one needs to leave. Agreed?"

They all nodded. Then Noah said, "I fear that the arts and sciences faculty do not view medicine as scholarship, though believe me, at Yale it is. Our clinicians know how very good our research scientists are. I've been building up research since I became dean. Our microbiologists deserve their national fame. Right now the pharmacology department is about to announce some stunning experiments using a new nerve drug on frogs and pigs. There's a potential cure for M.S. in the making, though right now the substance is primarily a dangerous poison. But Jerry, I'm no scholar. I'm a Jewish doctor and medical administrator. I spend evenings by preference with my wife and kids, not on the rubber chicken circuit raising money. So I don't consider myself a candidate. I'd like to stay on this committee unless one of you objects."

The others made reassuring noises. Noah continued. "One reason I want to stay with you is to join Professor Lee in making a case for science. Yale has to have a president who is literate about the sciences. The traditional emphasis on the humanities here won't do as the university approaches the twenty-first century."

"I'm not sure I agree," Jerry said. "We want the best possible president. That involves a lot of qualifications. I suppose literacy about science is desirable, but the King has built up science as much as you have, Noah, and he's a historian."

"He goes out of his way to consult scientists," Noah replied.

"Exactly," Jerry said. "Is consultation the same as literacy? If so, I agree. We don't want anyone who is anti-scientific."

"I'm afraid," Gordon said, "that humanists here grouse too much about science. Not you, Jerry, but many of your colleagues. The Yale atmosphere rains on science. We recruit kids because they are going to be physicists or biologists, they say, and by the end of their sophomore year, they decide the labs are too far away from the residential colleges, and their roommates think science is for weenies, so they switch to American Studies or some other gut major. That's what's worrying Noah and Charlie. They want a president who will change the undergraduate culture."

"Roger is right," Lilith said. "Yale students shun the sciences, by and large. Harvard is entirely different. I'm not sure any president can push a button and change the Yale mood, but we'd do well to find someone who wanted to. Anyway, bitching about science and the high costs of science is a kind of anti-intellectualism, so we certainly don't want someone who is against science."

"Obviously. Now let's go home and continue this discussion another day when we have more concrete matters before us," Jerry said.

"Okay," Charlie said, "but will my rule also apply to the Fellows' search committee? Is Senator Overman a candidate? She's on their committee. So is that bishop who's always struck me as ambitious beyond his abilities."

"I'll report your point to Proxmire Young," Jerry promised, "and let you know his response. May we go now?"

"Please God," Lilith said as they all started for the door. "Carter's here for the weekend and I can't wait to have lunch with him."

"I'll bet he can't wait either," Noah said. "Neither could I if I were your husband and could see that look in your eyes."

On that Saturday morning Prox Young and his committee held their first meeting in a private room at the Century Association on 43rd Street just west of Fifth Avenue in New York. Prox had suggested the Yale Club of New York as the site, but Charles Dray, the one alumni Fellow in the group, had warned him that the Yale Club was frequented by many of the faculty. The committee needed a more private place for meetings and later for interviewing candidates. Young knew Dray was right but he didn't much like him. The scion of an old New Haven family who yielded to no one in his opinions about the university and its policies, Dray, a prosperous lawyer, had waged a long campaign against Prox's own nominees to win election to the Corporation. Prox would have preferred an alumni Fellow more dependent on his leadership. Nor did Young much like Sis Overman. She had clashed with him years earlier when he had testified before the Senate Finance Committee of which she was then a member. She was far too eager, he felt, to curb the power of the Federal Reserve over interest rates, far too much a populist for his taste. But Young took solace from the presence of Bishop Peter Manning and Governor Billy Murphy. They were undistinguished, but a combination of piety and flattery would handle them.

Once they all had coffee and muffins at hand, Prox asked whether they were willing to assemble every fortnight as a committee, ordinarily in New York but in New Haven when the Fellows had a regular weekend meeting. Next he reviewed the letter to the alumni, which Tony Celotto had drafted for the committee's use. Tony, serving as secretary, broke in to observe that his secretary, Isabel Doughton, would arrange the necessary meetings. She would also, he said, type all minutes. He asked if anyone objected.

"Tony means the heavyweight who sits just outside his office and acts as his gatekeeper," Prox explained. "She's been there forever and never yet broken a confidence. She'll be safe in her role." No one objected.

Those matters arranged, discussion turned to definition of the qualities desirable in the next president. Charley Dray and Peter Manning believed that only Yale graduates should be considered, but the others agreed with Prox that the search should exclude no one. Without exception they considered experience with managing an educational institution, or some large part of one, a desirable qualification, though any relevant managerial track record might constitute a reasonable equivalent. Sis Overman alone placed an appreciation of scholarship and a dedication to preserving a scholarly environment high on her list of desiderata. The others were more concerned with finding a president capable of soothing the alumni. No one expressed concern about student opinion. The consensus, as Prox had expected, ran clearly against selecting another Arthur Stiles. Indeed only Sis Overman, whom the King had recruited for the corporation, cited his accomplishments as examples for his successor to emulate.

At that point they had been together for nearly an hour without any gossip about candidates. Billy Murphy started it. "Look here, guys and gal," he said, "it's all very well to talk about management experience and scholarly environments and alumni relations, but when push comes to shove, you know damn well that it will be the personal chemistry of the candidate that moves us. No two of us respond the same way to personal chemistry. As for me, I can tell you right now that fellow Humber strikes me as a cold fish. So I'm against him. My instincts are pretty good, too. But I've no sense of the other eligibles."

"You'll have a chance to meet them all and to interview those we put high on our list," Prox said.

"The Governor's point isn't procedural," Sis Overman interrupted, "it's substantive, and it's important. Chemistry does matter. It will probably prove decisive. That's why you won't pick a woman. None of you is really comfortable with women in command, so no woman will have the right chemistry. The same is true of blacks. Oh, Prox, I know. You're broad-minded. And you'll see to it that an African-American or an Asian-American and a woman are on the short list that you'll leak before we're done. But that won't be your private list. Your private list will be as WASP and male as you are, or maybe I should rephrase that—as this committee is."

"That's unfair, Senator," Prox replied. "We're too far away from a short list for anyone accurately to predict who will be on it."

"I'm predicting who won't," Sis said. "But I've said my piece. And don't get me wrong, gentlemen. I know the students put my name on their list, but I can't afford the job. The salary wouldn't pay my current income tax. And I could never get along with the faculty. Most of them are vainer and more contentious than I am."

"That's your pose," Prox said. "Actually you're a lady panda bear. But I think it's premature for us to start talking about candidates. Let's have some more input first from both alumni and faculty, and let's ask some prominent educators for suggestions of able men and women. I'll ask Arthur Stiles for the names of outstanding people to consult, and next time we meet, we can agree about whom to write and whom to see. Then we can divide the names among us and get started."

"You're right," Bishop Manning said, "but I want to say now that it will take a lot of persuading to make me believe that there's a better candidate out there somewhere than our own Eugene Barnard. He's a Christian gentleman and a fine author, and he's my man until someone proves otherwise."

"Please, Peter," Prox said, "let's hold off for now. As a matter of fact, let's adjourn. I so move."

Without replying the others stood up and began to leave. As they did, Charley Dray put his right arm around Bishop Manning's shoulders and said, "Barnard is a good man, Peter, but not quite as good as Bob Humber. I won't argue the point yet, but I hope you'll spend some time

53

with Bob so that you get to know him. You'll like him, I'm sure."

"You lawyers hang together, don't you?" Manning replied. "I'll do as you suggest, and you be sure to get to know Gene."

"He'll see to that, I'm told," Dray said as they all boarded the elevator to the ground floor.

Non-profit institutions of all kinds—hospitals, universities, charitable and research foundations, museums and symphony orchestras—face common legal problems peculiar to their status. To stimulate discussion of those problems, the Viney Foundation offered to underwrite the expenses of a committee selected by the New York bar. The Viney Foundation had been established by Desmond Viney, the founder of a successful software company that had merged with a computer giant, leaving him with wealth beyond his dreams. The foundation also subsidized a program to find and cultivate entrepreneurial genius. Its offer to the New York bar resulted in a conference of the committee and some invited friends at Viney Medical University, another of Desmond's charities, in Yonkers, a Westchester County suburb on the Hudson River just north of the Bronx. The non-profit study group assembled there on the very Saturday on which the Yale search committees met. The agenda called for a report about current legal difficulties in hospitals and medical schools from the Vice President of Viney University, Dr. Aaron Shapiro, who was also a leading endocrinologist, celebrated for his research on dwarfism.

As Shapiro noticed when he began to talk, there was only one woman in his audience of lawyers. Since she was most attractive, he wished he could identify her, but he had to admit to himself that he had never seen her before. Her bright red, woolen sheath set off her graying blond hair and eyes, and Shapiro, a widower who liked slim women with big noses like hers, gazed at her long enough for her to become aware of his attention before he made a conscious effort to focus on his text. He would meet her later, he promised himself. For now he had better try to explain something about hospitals and their legal problems to a group of lawyers who appeared so healthy and prosperous and unfamiliar with hospitals that every one of them probably still had his tonsils and vermiform appendix.

Shapiro was not entirely right. The committee he addressed consisted largely of academic lawyers, not practicing counselors. They were all personally comfortable but much less prosperous than he thought, and two of them had had stomach surgery. One of the few engaged fully in the practice of law was the woman he admired from the podium. Elizabeth Strafford, who was by no means rich, had driven to Yonkers that morning from her home in New Haven, an hour and a half away. She owed her place on the committee to her expertness in tax law and to her victory as pro bono counsel to the Fairfield School for Girls in its successful defense against a federal ruling requiring it to hire more male teachers. Elizabeth, her partners like to boast, had protected the virginity of a generation of suburban maidens by her victory in *U.S. v. Girls.*

As she sat apparently listening intently to Shapiro, she was in fact lost in reverie. She had already read his preliminary written report on the issues he was discussing. Secure in her memory of that document, she had turned her semi-consciousness to her problems with her husband. Gene Barnard, she now decided, was intolerable. She would leave him as soon as she conveniently could. To minimize gossip, she would have to wait until Yale was further along in its search for a new president, but she had been a fool, she told herself, to let Gene's threat deter her. The Goldstein marriage, she was sure, was strong enough to survive her one-nighter with Alan. And to hell with Gene!

Just then, to her surprise, everyone stood up. In her preoccupation, she had failed to notice that Shapiro had finished his presentation. The men were preparing to take a coffee break, so she arose and joined them. Sipping coffee out of the way of the others, Betty studied Shapiro who was talking to a group of lawyers gathered around him. No one, she reflected, would call him a handsome man. But he was certainly masculine—rather short, barrel-chested, with a head of shaggy white hair, black hairs protruding just a little from his nostrils and ears, heavy gray eyebrows that formed a thick line across his forehead, big teeth, a deep voice, and a remarkably gentle smile. He was wearing a brown tweed suit overlaid with a broad blue plaid, cut to the high-waisted style of Saville Row. An interesting looking man, she thought, blushing a little as he caught her eye and started toward her.

"Hello," he said as he reached her side and extended his hand. "I don't think we've met. I'm Aaron Shapiro from Viney University, but I don't know your name."

"I'm Elizabeth Strafford from my law firm in Bridgeport," Betty answered, shaking his hand. "I know who you are, and I was impressed by your analysis." Her glance at his left hand had revealed neither wristwatch nor wedding ring. That did not mean much, she mused. She didn't wear a ring, either. But it was a start. She wanted to know Shapiro better.

"Of course," he said. "Desmond Viney told me about you. Aren't you the lawyer who defended the girls' school against some kind of affirmative action order?"

"Guilty as charged," Betty replied, "but I'd rather be recognized as a hot-shot tax attorney. That's how I make my living."

"Miss Strafford," Shapiro said, "I shall think of you henceforth annually on April 15. Frankly, since we're chatting, I'll admit that I'd like to think of you more often than that. Would you consider a drink with me after we adjourn this afternoon? I'm very tame, and I know a quiet cocktail lounge in Dobbs Ferry, the next town to us."

"Yes," Betty said, she hoped not too quickly. "I'll be glad to join you. They're heading back to their chairs again, so we had better go, too. But I'll look for you after the meeting." She was much more eager for that moment, she realized, than she had any right to be.

ISABEL

Tony Celotto's notes and Jerry Walsh's laconic summary of the first meetings of the search committees disappointed Isabel when she read them on Monday. She learned from them nothing she did not already know. Still, they confirmed the news stories that put Barnard and Humber ahead in the presidential sweepstakes. That information suited her purposes. She would ask around about the Barnard marriage. She had suspected for some time that there was some scandal there. More important, the moment had obviously come to press Humber. He had had a chance to think over her first note. Now some cash would be useful. She would not ask for all she wanted at once. Two bites would be more effective, a smaller piece now, a larger piece soon. She had made the necessary preparations. So before leaving her office in the later afternoon, alone and with her computer screen in front of her, she wrote her next note:

> *You surely have not forgotten my earlier message. I want old bills, unmarked, fifty fifties, twenty twenties, ten tens. You can afford them. Pack them carefully in a brown manila envelope and mail them special delivery, insured by not registered, to Snoopy, P.O. Box 9026, New Haven, 06533. That will pay for your bra and panties. I'll bill you later for your wife's cane and uniform. I'll expect the package no later than next Thursday. Otherwise I'll compose a letter to Harry*

Grayson of the Yale Daily News over the following weekend. He's eager to promote Professor Barnard for president.

4.
CANDIDATES

The search for a successor to Arthur Stiles excited many ambitions. For Gene Barnard and Bob Humber, it opened the way to appointment to an office to which both men, self-consciously rivals, had long aspired. For Isabel Doughton it provided access to minutes of the search committees, access that she exploited for her personal gain. For Harry Grayson, who dreamed of fame as an investigative reporter, it promised a chance for a first important scoop.

Now in the fall term of his senior year, Grayson looked forward to a career in journalism. He saw himself following in the steps of his three heroes, Walter Lippmann, David Brinkley and Bob Woodward. He expected by age thirty to have a Sunday morning talk show of his own on a major television network. Toward that goal he had devoted much of his energy since his freshman year to the *Yale Daily News*, of which he had become managing editor the previous spring. Harry strode briskly as he walked from the *News* building on York Street to Woodbridge Hall. He was on his way to an important appointment where he could place a rumor from which he planned to make a first strike toward fame. He knew a plausible rumor had to have some basis in truth. Therefore his mission.

"Come in Harry," Isabel Doughton called out when Harry knocked on her office door. "Mr. Celotto is expecting you. Go on through to his office."

"I also want to see you," Harry said. "I've a question. Is it true that Vice President Bush will visit Yale next month? And if so, can I arrange an interview with him?"

"Harry, you've been around long enough to know you'll have to ask Mr. Celotto that kind of question."

"Well then, is it true that you're transcribing the minutes of the Fellows' search committee and of the faculty committee, too? I suppose they're confidential."

"You know they're confidential," Isabel said. "Just what are you after, you rascal?"

"I plead innocent," Harry replied, "and I'll try Mr. Celotto now."

Tony Celotto greeted Harry warmly. "Hi there, brother in Loaf and Blade. What's on your mind?"

"Just wondered if George Bush was visiting Yale next month," Harry said. "Rumor has it that he is, and that the visit is to test his candidacy for the Yale presidency. That must get Dean Humber's goat."

"Be off with you," Tony said. "You're fishing and I won't bite. When there's news you'll get it when everyone else does." He turned to his desk and Harry left.

The next morning the *Yale Daily News* printed a leader: "BUSH DUE HERE?" Following Harry's byline, the story began, "Rumors in the office of the Secretary of the University put Vice President Bush at Yale next month officially to visit the college, his alma mater, but unofficially to explore the Yale presidency as a possibility when his term ends in Washington. The same rumors suggest that Dean Humber, a leading candidate for the same position, is not pleased...neither Tony Celotto not Miss Doughton, his executive secretary, would confirm the rumors."

Tony Celotto called Harry at the *News* and read him the riot act, but Harry didn't mind, for the *New Haven Register* picked up the story and his byline, and the *Washington Post* used both. It was a first for him with the *Post.*

Proxmire Young bridled when he read Harry's piece. He telephoned Jerry Walsh who assured him that the story was constructed of gossamer. "The kid doesn't know any better," Jerry said.

"The kid is a menace," Prox replied. "If we select anyone from public life, he'll have to be a lot less silly than Bush. I think I'll call the *News* and say so."

"Hold on," Jerry advised. "It would be a mistake to ask any public figure to be president of Yale. That would send a message Yale shouldn't send. It would suggest that the Fellows consider the academy bankrupt. You shouldn't suggest that because it's not true. And because you should take pains not to feed the prejudice of Tory alumni who believe the academy is monopolized by incompetent left-wing intellectuals."

"Isn't it?" Prox asked sourly.

"I'm serious," Jerry replied. "Please consider telling the *Yale Daily* that you will turn only to academic candidates, here or elsewhere, and will exclude all members of both search committees."

"We've agreed to the latter, as you know," Prox said. "We might as well agree to the former. But you and I have to have a private talk about politics someday."

"OK," Jerry said. "How about after the search is over?"

"I'll do it your way," Prox promised, "but I'll wring Grayson's neck when next I see him."

Harry Grayson's story had irritated Tony Celotto who found it irresponsible, as it was. The story confirmed Isabel Doughton's opinion of Harry as potentially useful for her purposes. Any leak she gave him he would surely convert into headlines, as Dean Humber would realize when she next threatened him. The story at first infuriated Robert Humber who considered Bush too liberal and therefore a national disaster. But on reflection, Humber concluded that the more rumors in circulation, and the more outlandish they were, the less he had to worry about "Snoopy." He had no intention of yielding to blackmail. His tastes in sex were his own business, and his only. But if "Snoopy" decided to go public, no one would pay much heed to still more unconfirmed gossip. Indeed Humber felt a perverse gratitude to Harry Grayson for the commotion he had generated.

Nevertheless Humber considered the time propitious for rounding up his own conservative supporters. They would be as furious as he was that rumors put Bush close to 43 Hillhouse, the president's residence. Accordingly he called Archibald Mound, one of the alumni Fellows and an ideologue who shared his right wing views. Mound, a large man with a quick intelligence that belied his reputation as a jock, was a graduate of Yale College and Law School. He had been an all American halfback as an undergraduate, then an editor of the law journal, and later a founder of a Chicago think-tank for conservative intellectuals. A resident of Evanston, he served as a recruiter of Chicago area alumni who organized to oppose and contradict Arthur Stiles' liberal statements about public issues. The King took pains not to implicate the university, but the media considered the man and the institution as one. Mound's group operated to control that misapprehension. In frequent letters to newspaper editors Humber served as spokesman for that endeavor.

Conservative alumni votes had elected Mound to the Yale Corporation. There, as an alumni Fellow, he had kept a low profile, awaiting the day when an issue would arise on which he could focus. The presidential search gave him the chance he wanted. He would do all he could to advance the Humber cause. Now the two allies decided to enlist Charles Dray as their man on the search committee. Mound would get Dray to ask Humber to describe his vision for Yale. Then Dray could be counted on to sell that vision to the others on the committee while Mound organized a letter-writing campaign on Humber's behalf.

Flattered when Mound called him, Dray arranged an appointment with Humber, who welcomed him to his grandiose office several days later. "You know, Bob," Dray said after they had exchanged pleasantries, "many of the law alumni want to see you become president, and some of the conservatives among them have asked me to talk with you about your ideas about Yale. You should also be aware that the faculty advisory committee is determined to recommend no one hostile to or ignorant of science. Are you okay on that issue?"

"I read the usual news about science," Humber said. "But I'm no expert in any science. As an undergraduate I had high grades in the science courses I took, just as I did in all my courses. I had a year of geology and two years of math. I'd like to know more than I do about physics and genetics, and I'd like those fields to get continuing support here. I also believe every undergraduate should devote at least four semester courses to science or math, and I don't mean biology for poets. How's that for an answer?"

"Great," Dray replied. "But I guess I also have to ask you about your reputation for extravagance, especially in furnishings."

"When we raise money for the Law School," Humber said, "we always announce that some of it is for current use. The donors know that up front. Some of the funds go for research by faculty or students. Some goes for amenities. Those amenities include my office. After all, Charley, successful alumni are accustomed to elegance and expect it of their dean. They swoon over my office, which puts them in the right mood. I can't afford to be shabby, so I spend freely on my office, my clothing, my residence. Men of my stature have no choice."

"I take your point," Dray said. "Would you go on about the Yale presidency?"

"I must admit," Humber said, "that I will not defer to Proxmire Young and his claque. If elected, I mean to do things my way. I have deep reservations about affirmative action. I'm not much interested in finding black coaches and women deans. I'm an unabashed elitist. I want the best and the brightest in every position, and that still means mostly white men."

"We're all for talent," Dray said, meekly. He was sure that Humber's position would offend the faculty committee, but some of the Fellows would be pleased.

"I tell you, Charley," the dean went on, "I'd like to remake Yale College. I'd like to impose a curriculum based on the educational principles of Cardinal Newman. That would be a triumph."

"Good Lord, Bob," Dray said, "you take my breath away." He was not sure what Cardinal Newman stood for, but he was impressed by Humber.

Humber nodded. "I do that to a lot of callers." Then the dean arose and showed Charley gently to the door. Charley went along peaceably.

Jerry Walsh left his office in a hurry to arrive on time for his scheduled luncheon with Lilith Furman and Richard Mason, the former provost. Jerry had reserved for their use the pit at Branford College, the residential college of which he was a fellow. The pit, down a few stairs from the back of the Branford dining hall, afforded quiet and privacy, both important for the discussion they were planning. Just looking at Branford College picked up Jerry's mood, as it always did. Yale assigned its undergraduates to twelve residential colleges, each a center for its members' living, dining and socializing. Two of the colleges were more or less neo-colonial. One was neo-Gothic on the outside and neo-colonial around the inner court. Of the rest, all collegiate Gothic or a modern facsimile thereof, arguably the most beautiful architecturally was Branford.

At the east end of Branford's great court rose Harkness Tower, modeled after the Boston Stump, the tower of a small English Gothic cathedral. The Branford tower housed carillon bells, which were playing a Bach organ prelude as Jerry entered through the west gate. The tower and the wing lying to its north came at once into his view. The grass in the court extending toward him was still green enough to contrast vividly with the paths surrounding and intersecting it. The impact of the scene, washed with music, gave Jerry a familiar satisfaction as he turned into the entry leading to the common room and through it to the stairs to the Hall. Moving on into the buttery, Jerry picked up a tray, some cutlery and a paper napkin, and selected from the steam table a cheeseburger, a glass of milk, and some cookies. Nodding to students he knew as he walked through the Hall, he descended the stairs to the pit where Dick Mason and Lilith awaited him.

At Jerry's request, Dick Mason had agreed to interrupt his research, even though he was on leave, to talk about Yale's financial problems. A quiet, orderly, self-contained man, he had made himself an expert on the economics of higher education. After an exchange of greetings, he began. "All major universities, public or private, have similar financial problems, basically containing costs and increasing income. But to address those matters you don't need an economist or investment banker. You do need someone prepared to consult financial managers and to hire a vice president, perhaps two or three, to manage the university's finances, to spur development, and to strengthen internal administration. Let me elaborate." He stopped for a moment and ate what was left of his cottage cheese and salad. He then continued for half an hour. "So Yale and other universities," Dick concluded, "are going to have to reduce the number of tenured faculty and earn more money from private research grants, largely in the hot sciences. That prospect may run against Yale tradition, but we're reaching the point where tradition has to yield to the needs of the future. You will find that President Stiles agrees with that analysis though he would not like to initiate the changes. That helps to explain his decision to resign."

"Sounds heavy," Lilith commented.

"Would you like more detail?" Dick asked.

"I'm sated," Jerry replied. "I think we've got the picture. I hope you explain it all to Proxmire Young and the others."

"Prox knows enough to do that himself," Dick said. "The next president has to go into office with his eyes open. And I must return to my rock pile for an afternoon of labor. Good luck to you both." So saying, he departed.

"He knows what to do," Lilith said, "and he has the guts to do it. Why shouldn't he be the next president?"

"Because he really doesn't want to be," Jerry replied. "He's a shy man, uncomfortable as a speaker, very private, sort of an intimate intellectual. He knows us well enough to relax with us. He's rather remote with people he knows less well."

"I'm going to keep him on my private list anyhow," Lilith said. "He's more cosmopolitan than Gene Barnard and much more modest than my arrogant dean. But look at the time, Jerry! I must leave, too." Jerry rose and they walked out together.

Her responsibilities as a member of the Fellows' search committee weighed heavily on Sis Overman. She felt a strong loyalty to Yale and its Law School where she had first met and wrestled with abstract ideas, and where her male classmates, to her surprise and gratification, had elected her to the law journal. Her experience as a law student launched her on her career and persuaded her that she could compete successfully with talented and competitive men. Because she believed that Yale deserved skillful, steady, innovative leadership, she admired Arthur Stiles, and she worried about the inadequacies of her colleagues. She considered Governor Murphy and Bishop Manning lightweights, and she had reservations about Charley Dray's judgment. That left her essentially alone, as she saw it, to serve as a counterweight to Proxmire Young. She knew that Young favored Gene Barnard to succeed the King, but she had always found Barnard superficial, just as she had found Robert Humber rigid and authoritarian. So she was eager to look beyond internal candidates, and she sensed that among the faculty advisory group, Dean Noah Montefiore had similar leanings.

Sis was delighted therefore when Noah called her one evening to ask whether she could meet him for breakfast the next morning at the Hotel Washington. He was taking the early airplane from New Haven in order to testify before a Senate committee investigating the use of radioactive isotopes in gastrointestinal diseases. A recent accident had led to the death of a patient at a veterans' hospital and an ensuing brouhaha involving the American Legion. Noah was due on the Hill at about 10:30, so a nine o'clock breakfast would give him and Sis a chance to exchange views about the Yale search.

Sis had only orange juice for breakfast so she talked while Noah attacked his stack of buckwheat pancakes with grits on the side. "So you see," she said as she finished describing her concerns, "I'm dubious about Barnard and poisonous toward Humber. Indeed I've come to your conclusion. I think we should be looking at some research scientists with administrative experience."

"Yale scientists?" Noah asked, his mouth full of the last of the pancakes.

"Among others, I suppose," Sis replied. "But must you find a Yale professor or alumnus? Blue is not the only color of the ocean."

"I don't need to be told that," Noah said. "Our committee, however, has yet to generate any suggestions of scientists with the other qualities we're seeking."

"You must know some," Sis said. "Don't be bashful about your professional peers, certainly not with me. I want to know about them."

"I'm not a scientist," Noah reminded her, "though I know and work with lots of scholars in the medical and biological sciences. Right this minute one name springs to mind. He's Aaron Shapiro, the vice president of Viney Medical University. He's published some stunning research on dwarfism, and he's been a consultant in our neurological work on M.S. But he's a Jew, if that matters."

"Not to me," Sis replied, "but then I'm a woman, which for Prox Young is certainly worse. I'll put Shapiro's name on the Fellows' list. It won't sway Gene Barnard's fans, but it's certainly worth exploring. Please send me any information you have about Shapiro and about anyone else you think of."

"I promise," Noah said, swallowing some coffee. "Shapiro's a widower with two boys, but I see no significance in that. Are we done? If I leave now, I'll have time to walk to the Hill. After this breakfast, I need the exercise."

"Be gone with you," Sis said. "When I feel the urge to exercise, I sit down. And thanks."

Montefiore was a Jew himself, she remembered as he disappeared. She'd put his name on her list, too. That would serve at least to rankle Proxmire Young.

ISABEL

As September ended and October began, the search for a new president seemed to slip into lower gear. The Fellows' committee continued to receive suggestions from alumni, and to discuss and discard most of them. Interviews with possible candidates were also underway, but not since Sis Overman had recommended Dr. Shapiro had any outsider won plaudits. The chancellor of a major state system in the South, a man reputed to be a sterling administrator, had nothing to propose about higher education that Sis Overman and Prox Young, who had dinner with him, had not heard better said before. Prox and Bishop Manning found the youthful dean of an Ivy League arts and sciences faculty as banal as the King had predicted he would be. Governor Murphy and Charley Dray spent an hour with the president of one of the "heavenly seven" women's colleges who was so uptight that both of them urged Sis Overman to declare her own availability if a woman had to be on the final list.

The resulting cryptic reports and minutes, all of which Isabel Doughton typed, left her feeling as empty as the committees did. They felt they were making little progress and began to think about focusing on the several men they had been considering for some time. She knew she was failing to find a new victim for Snoopy. Worse, Robert Humber continued to ignore her. Peeved by his inattention and frustrated in her desire for the jewelry, Isabel decided to buy the emerald brooch at once, drawing down her savings account for that purpose, and then to replenish her funds by getting at Humber through Harry Grayson at the *Yale Dailey News*.

AN OLD BLUE CORPSE:
A NEW HAVEN MYSTERY

Isabel's mood soared when the brooch arrived from Cartier. She could almost feel her father's hands pinning it on her dark blue dinner gown. In her mirror the deep blue of the gown admirably set off the glimmering green of the brooch. With growing excitement she put on her father's academic regalia to see the contrast of the blue in it with the blue of the dress. But before she could proceed, she remembered that she had yet to arrange to meet Harry Grayson. Aware that Newsies worked late at the paper, she called him there. She implied that she might talk to him off the record if he dropped by her office the next afternoon. He said he would. But when she returned to her mirror, the moment had passed, her mood had shifted again, and pouting, she changed into a roomy caftan and put the brooch safely away in her dresser drawer.

With Harry soon due to arrive, the next afternoon Isabel surmised that he was probably an innocent about sex. She would have to test him before revealing anything about Humber. Her surmise was correct. Harry had read some recommended books but still considered a good-night kiss a sexual triumph, and he had had few enough of those. His naiveté and her caution were to make communication awkward. But full of hope when Harry appeared, Isabel began bravely.

"You must wonder why I suggested you come to see me," she said. "I'm worried about the presidential search. I can't read the minutes to you, but off the record, I wonder what you would think, Harry, if you learned that a leading candidate was a sex pervert."

"You mean gay?" Harry asked. "That's not supposed to matter."

Isabel paused. It had mattered in her youth. Where did today's undergraduates get their ideas? "No," she replied. "I mean a kinky perversion, a foot fetish for example."

"Oh, there was a foot nibbler loose in the library stacks last year," Harry said. "I wrote a piece about him. One night he nibbled the foot of a woman graduate student who had kicked off her shoe. It happened on the ninth floor, and no one heard her scream. He ran away. After she reported the incident and I wrote it up, several other women came along with a similar story, but they never caught him."

"No," Isabel said impatiently. "I mean like a foot fetish but worse."

"Hey," Harry said, "it doesn't really matter. Professor Barnard will get the job. Or are you trying to tell me something about him? Whatever it is, it won't change my mind, I'll say that." He stood up, frowned at Isabel and departed.

Damn, Isabel said to herself. She could not depend on juvenile messengers, for if Harry was an example of the breed, they were so laid back about sexual practices that they wouldn't take her bait. The Fellows would feel differently, she was sure, but Humber seemed willing to risk their response. She needed either to shake him or to locate another target. She would press her inquiries about the Barnard marriage, she decided, and think about how to attack Humber through his wife, who would surely want to keep her sadomasochism private. To hell with Harry, she told herself while she reached for another chocolate chip cookie.

5.
PAIRINGS

The second Saturday in October Lilith Furman and Carter Jefferson were giving a dinner party. Lilith, eager to get Carter out of the house that afternoon, arranged for him to join Jerry Walsh at the Yale Bowl for the Colgate game. Yale won with ease, to Jerry's delight. Carter was pleased less by the outcome than by Jerry's obvious joy. Their high spirits still prevailed when the Walshes arrived for dinner, as shortly thereafter did Tony Celotto with Lucy Guglielmi, an English teacher at the Hopkins Grammar School to whom he was engaged. Cocktails had just begun when conversation turned, predictably, to the presidential search. Tony, Lilith and Jerry tried hard to avoid indiscretions, but the others gently prodded them for news. The prodding continued off and on through dinner and beyond.

It was Tony who broke down. "I don't see why, off the record and in this room, we can't admit that Gene Barnard is ahead of the pack. After all, you must suspect that Proxmire Young would not have it any other way."

"That's enough, Tony," Lilith interrupted. "Let's not go on."

"Lilith's right," Jerry said. "We know how curious you all are, but we are bound to confidentiality."

"Agreed," Tony said. "I should confess, however, as I have to Lucy, that I suspect my name is on one list, and I would love the job. But I'm not going to get it. A master's degree isn't enough. I have no vote, of course, but if I did I'd take seriously the gossip that has Sis Overman

71

on some private lists. Isabel Doughton practically glowed when she learned that a woman had a chance. Small chance, I told her. She can hardly wait for the minutes of the committee meetings. If one of you is overwhelmed by curiosity, try bribing Isabel."

Lilith, deliberately creating a diversion, interrupted again by asking Carter whether he had watched the football game or Jerry's reactions to it. Carter had found Jerry more interesting, he said, than Ivy League football. Conversation moved then to gastronomy, a favorite subject of everyone there, and continued until Jerry suggested at eleven that the time had come to say farewell.

Later, in bed, Karen, snuggling close to Jerry, said quietly, "The speculation tonight reminded me of something about Gene I think you should know. I've known for some time but have hesitated to tell you."

"I'm all ears, but don't take too long. I've other plans," Jerry said, moving still closer to her.

"Not long after term began," Karen continued, "one morning about ten, I went over to Sylvia Wheatley's house for a stick of butter. You know that she and I wander in and out of each other's kitchen. Well, I started for her kitchen and walked past the doorway to the living room. I didn't mean to peek, but I could not help seeing Sylvia on the sofa, her eyes closed and her skirt up to her waist, with Gene kneeling on the floor in front of her with his face in her middle. I turned and left as quietly as I could, but she must have seen me before I got out. A few days later she talked casually about Gene and asked me to keep her up to date about his chances for the presidency. A week or so later she called one afternoon and came over for a long heart-to-heart."

"Wanted to compare notes about good sex, did she?" Jerry asked.

"Be serious," Karen commanded. "Don't interrupt! She wanted to tell me about her relationship with Gene. They met one day while shopping for groceries. He looked sort of down, so she asked him to have a cup of coffee when he got back to his house, almost next door to hers, after all. He did. They began to talk. She was sympathetic. One thing led to another, and they ended up in bed. Morning coffee has ended that way regularly since."

"What's the problem, then?" Jerry asked. "We all know that Gene and Betty have had trouble since they lost that baby."

"That's what Gene told Sylvia about," Karen said. "Sylvia's crazy about him. Says he's the gentlest lover in the world. She had been living a virginal life since Seth's death almost ten years ago, and Gene has bowled her over. She sees only his side of things and blames Betty for the abortion. Of course that baby would have been a monster, but Sylvia, who's never had children, can't understand that. Gene told her he'd been impotent since the loss of the baby, though Sylvia has obviously cured that. Anyway, they want to get married but Gene is afraid of any scandal until after the Fellows pick a new president."

"Divorce is no scandal," Jerry said. "Not any longer. But an affair with a neighbor might be. Can't you persuade Sylvia to get Gene to explain his feelings to Betty?"

"It's not that simple," Karen replied. "Gene is afraid that Betty would be vindictive. The way Sylvia tells it, he's threatened to reveal some affair of hers. He's even had her followed. He knows she's a lush but can't get her off the sauce. He's caught between two fears. He's afraid of what she may do while she's his wife, and he's afraid of what she may do if he moves toward divorce. He's really afraid that, either way, she'll wreck his chances to be president."

"Okay, I'll talk to him myself," Jerry said. "We've been friends for years. I'll try over a beer after our next squash match. He and Betty would both be better off if they do get divorced. And I hope a divorce will not be a decisive factor in the Yale sweepstakes. You work on Sylvia."

"I'll give it a shot," Karen replied. "She cares deeply about his ambitions. She's sort of motherly toward him. After all, she's older than he by some seven years."

"Well, I don't want you to be motherly tonight," Jerry said.

"Try me," Karen replied.

The next afternoon, after Gene Barnard had fallen asleep watching a Giants' football game, Betty Barnard telephoned her law partner, Alan Goldstein. "Sorry to bother you on a Sunday," Betty said when he answered, "but we have to talk."

"Why not right now?" Alan replied. "I'm alone here. The others have gone for a walk in East Rock Park to see the foliage."

"Alan," Betty said, "I've been thinking about our one-nighter. To be honest, Gene has more or less been threatening to tell Hanna about it unless I toe the line he's drawn. I can't live with that any longer. I'm bent double with guilt about Hanna, and I've got to tell her that you and I were in our cups and made a dumb mistake. Confession is good for the soul, I guess, but I don't want to complicate your marriage, so I need your advice."

"Relax, Betty," Alan said. "I told her what happened the very next day. I apologized for my amorous inebriation. I promised it wouldn't happen again, with you or with anyone else. She took it pretty well."

"I feel myself turning beet red," Betty said. "How can I ever face her? What did she say?"

"To quote her exactly," Alan replied, "she said, 'Damn you, Alan. You're an absolute shit. Maybe an honest shit, but just keep away from me for a few weeks while I practice hating you.' The few weeks aren't yet over, I've discovered, but things have begun to ease, and believe me, I won't make that mistake again. Hanna blames me, not you. She says the man is always at fault. So you can relax. You and I would do well to forget the whole episode. We had too much to drink. Things got away from us. We'll stay sober in the future. And you don't need to talk it over with Gene. We don't want his opinion about this."

"Good advice," Betty said. "I needed a smart lawyer and I found one. Thanks. I'll see you in the office tomorrow. Should I talk to Hanna soon?"

"I think she feels less said, sooner mended," Alan said. "I'd say nothing. When next you happen to meet her, treat her as if nothing had happened. She wants to forget it, and so do I."

"And so do I," Betty said. "Thanks. I feel much better."

Betty leaned back in her chair. Now, she thought, she was free to tell Gene she wanted to end their charade. But her sense of guilt extended to him. She did not want to hurt him or his chances to become president of Yale. Perhaps, she mused, she should consult Karen Walsh, surely her best friend. Karen would know from Jerry what was going on at Yale. And Karen was a sensitive woman, a poet who wrote love sonnets. Betty could safely tell her about Aaron Shapiro, too.

Betty had no sooner put down the phone than it rang, awakening Gene, who picked up in his study. "I'm in New Haven, staying with the King," Proxmire Young said. "He and Charlotte have gone to visit some friend in the hospital, so I'm alone. Can you come down and join me for a drink? Come as you are. I'm in a sweater."

Gene said he'd be right there, called Betty to tell her he was going out, and arrived at 43 Hillhouse in less than ten minutes. Prox let him in and beckoned him to the study to the right of the front door. "What are you drinking?" Prox asked. "I'm into Arthur's good scotch."

"Great," Gene replied, "I'll have the same. Lots of rocks, please." He needed a drink, he thought to himself. He could not imagine why Proxmire Young had summoned him so suddenly.

"Gene," Prox said, handing him his drink, "we've got to talk. I'm telling you now, up front, that you're my candidate to succeed Arthur. That doesn't mean you have the job. It does mean that I've been inquiring about you, and I have a couple of questions, important questions. One's educational. One's personal."

"Go right ahead," Gene replied, more anxious than he let on. "I'm flattered and delighted that you favor me, and I have nothing to hide."

"Thank you," Prox said. "First, some of your colleagues think you're hostile to science. Can you reassure me about that matter."

"I have to plead guilty," Gene said, "to relative ignorance. But I'm trying to learn about the biological and medical sciences. That's why I was so eager to accept appointment as the humanist member on the Divisional Committee on the Biological Sciences. Just now I'm trying to follow discussions in that committee about pending proposals for tenure appointments in molecular biology. Believe me, the articles the candidates have published in learned journals are tough going for a layman. And I'm on a subcommittee on safety procedures in the labs at the medical school. We're scheduled to visit a lab where a couple of researchers have been doing something with animal muscles, something Dean Montefiore is excited about. It all has to do with sodium channels, apparently red-hot stuff. So you see, I'm learning."

"You strike me as sound about science," Prox said.

"Thanks," Gene said. "I appreciate your confidence."

"There's more," Prox said. "I'm sorry to bring it up, but half of New Haven seems to think your wife is a bit of a lush. The other half hints that she's sleeping around. How about it? We can't have any scandal at 43 Hillhouse."

"I'm sorry the question has had to come up," Gene replied, now more anxious than ever. He sipped his drink to buy time. "Look," he then said, "Betty and I have had problems since we lost a baby. I guess that's no secret. We've had words about her drinking. She's promised to try harder to control it. What else can I say?"

"You had better do something," Prox advised. "Put a chain around her. Make her behave for the next couple of months at least or she'll kill your chances. And keep her out of strange beds."

"I'll do what I can," Gene said. "She's a pretty independent woman."

"In that case, if she persists in her ways," Prox said brusquely, "perhaps you'd better let it be known that you intend to divorce her. Divorce is not a plus with the Fellows, but it's a damn sight better than alcoholism or adultery. And if she can't be Caesar's wife, you better be above reproach yourself. Live like a monk until this search is over. Now the King will be back any minute, so you had better get out of here. But clean up your wife's act or she'll destroy your future. I'm sorry to have to put it that way, but that's the way it is."

"You can count on me," Gene replied with far more apparent confidence than he felt. "Thanks for your candor."

They shook hands as Gene left, his heart racing. He wondered if Prox's remark about living like a monk meant that somehow the senior Fellow had learned about Sylvia Wheatley. Gene dreaded the risk of losing Sylvia, who had become just about indispensable to his life. But he also wanted desperately to become president of Yale.

He would have to be very careful to see Sylvia only when no one could observe them together. Sylvia would understand, but she wouldn't like it. And he would have to keep Betty under control. That had never been easy. Still, Prox was on his side, enough so to warn him. That was an encouraging omen.

October is a busy month in the academic world. The fall term, five or six weeks old, has gained momentum, with the novelty of the new year gone and courses demanding the full attention of students and faculty alike. As always in October, Jerry Walsh found his life too full. Karen was also under pressure, for she had her first book of poetry, the fruit of a decade of hard work, due at the Wesleyan University press at the end of November. Consequently neither of them could fit in the serious talks they meant to have with the Barnards.

On the third Saturday of the month, at the King's urging, Jerry joined him and Gene Barnard at the Bowl to see Yale play Columbia. Karen begged off and settled down to revise several lines in a long lyric poem she had written five years earlier. She had barely begun when Betty Barnard rang the front door bell, walked in, and called up the stairs to ask whether Karen could possibly spare her half an hour. As Karen started down, Betty explained from the foot of the stairs that she knew she was interrupting the muse, but she had a pressing matter to discuss. At first annoyed that she had a visitor, Karen responded to Betty's explanation and embraced her with genuine warmth before they repaired to the kitchen for coffee and cookies, their usual snack for exchanging confidences.

"It's been too long," Betty said as she nibbled on a Milano cookie. "I've been eager to talk to you for weeks. It's about Gene and me, and I really have to let my hair down. Have you time for that?"

"Betty, dear, you look so grim," Karen said, pouring coffee from an electric percolator, which had been keeping it warm. "Of course I have time for you. Always. I know you two have been having a rough stretch, and I've wanted to talk to you. Is something special the matter?"

"Nothing new, really, but I've been coming to my senses and seeing old problems in a different light," Betty said. "I guess everyone knows that our marriage has been rocky. But I am not a murderess. Gene admits as much when he wants to, but he tortures me with nasty accusations most of the time, that is, when we talk to each other at all. Really most of the time we avoid each other. We haven't had sex since I returned from the hospital. Gene tried a few times but with no enthusiasm or success. Then we both gave up. I admit I've been drinking too much and fallen into the wrong beds a few nights. Gene tried to blackmail me about it, to force me to make it seem our marriage was okay until a new president is chosen. He's obsessed about the appointment."

"Betty, please, you don't have to go on this way," Karen said. "All your friends know you've been having a rotten time. But blackmail is rather much."

"That's just the point. I'm not going to go on this way," Betty said. "I've made up my mind. Gene can go to hell. Oh, that's not fair. I've been no saint. But I'm moving out, and I'm going to get a divorce. If he doesn't like it, too bad!"

"Betty, he'll let you go, I'm sure," Karen said. "I should probably not tell you this, but I know he's been seeing another woman. I've been planning to tell you, and Jerry was planning to talk sense to Gene. We've just been so busy."

"Another woman! The hypocritical bastard!" Betty exclaimed. "I don't give a damn with whom he sleeps, but I sure resent his unloading on me when he's cheating himself. Who is the unfortunate girl?"

"Let Gene tell you that," Karen said. "Why not have a quiet talk with him? It's past time you both came to your senses. Then you can move out. A divorce shouldn't destroy Gene's chances, though it won't help them. And he could tell the Fellows, if they ask, that he's going to remarry, as I think he will."

"You're right," Betty said. "I just have to swallow what's left of my pride. I was coming to the same conclusion, but there's a related problem."

"What's that, if I may ask?"

"To tell the whole truth, Karen," Betty admitted, "there's another man, though he may not yet know how strongly I feel. I met him only about a month ago. We've had a long drink together, then a week later an intimate dinner in New York. We talked and talked and talked. I told him about the baby, and a little about Gene, and about my boozing. He told me about the death of his wife—melanoma, it was quick, and about the difficulties of raising two sons, and how he had to give up most of his research to get a regular schedule by turning to administration. When we left the restaurant we fell into each other's arms.

"Last weekend we stayed together at the inn in Washington, Connecticut. He's wonderful, and acts as if he cares about me, but when he learns all about me he may not be interested in me any longer. He hasn't proposed or anything like that, but he's great in bed, and I want him to love me. His life is complicated. Believe it or not, Yale has been in touch with him about the presidency! No offer, you understand, just some preliminary conversations. He has ambiguous feelings about Yale, I gather. But I feel torn. A divorce may hurt Gene. I don't want that. My liaison with another man may damage them both. I'd like a year in outer space. But I guess I'll have to level with them. It won't be easy. I've certainly made a mess of my life."

"You should forget about Yale and do what's good for you," Karen advised. "If you love the guy, you have to be totally honest with him. If he loves you, he won't hold your past indiscretions against you. Who is this new flame, or should I not ask?"

"I'll tell you," Betty said, "if you'll tell me who's playing house with Gene, and if you'll keep a secret, which I know you will."

"Telling you about Gene's affair would break a confidence," Karen said.

"I'll have to ask Gene, then," Betty said. "But I'll tell you anyhow. I'm bursting to tell someone. But don't let on even to Jerry. My guy's a vice president at Viney University, a sturdy, beautifully hairy, handsome Jewish doctor, pretty famous, named Aaron Shapiro."

"Shapiro," Karen said. "He must be the doctor Jerry recently met. He certainly is on the list for Yale. That is a complication. What a coincidence!"

ISABEL

Arthur Stiles, eager to facilitate the search for his successor, decided to give an informal luncheon at which the Fellows conducting that search could mingle with the faculty on the advisory committee. It would do them all good, he believed, to get to know each other better. He enlisted Tony Celotto to take charge of the preparations, and Tony asked Isabel Doughton to assist him. That task, he told her, would involve supervising Mary Murphy and her staff who were to cater the affair, scheduled for the following Saturday in the common room in the Hall of Graduate Studies.

Isabel was overjoyed. She expected her practiced skills as an eavesdropper to bring her up-to-date on the latest gossip. The occasion, she was sure, would end her long drought. It would allow her to reap the information that the guests sowed. In her upbeat mood, she bought a new dress, high at the neck, pleated from waist to ankle, a gown that flowed, a slimming black. She celebrated by devouring two chocolate éclairs.

6.
TEMPERAMENTS

On the Friday preceding the luncheon Arthur Stiles had planned, Charles Dray sat, drumming his fingers on his desk, as he waited for Proxmire Young to come to the telephone. Young's secretary had put Dray on hold almost five minutes earlier and he did not like waiting. He also suspected that Young was not above asserting his authority by making him wait. Dray had news of importance that deserved, he felt, more considerate treatment. He was about to hang up and see whether Young would call him back when he heard the phone on the receiving end hit a hard surface.

"Damn, I dropped the telephone," Prox said. "I'm sorry. It's hectic this morning. The market has been having fits, the yen is down again, and some of our clients are needlessly scared. Sorry that I couldn't get to the phone sooner. Dropped it because I was rushing. What's on your mind, Charley?"

Feeling appeased, Dray replied, "I'm sorry to bother you at a busy time, Prox. Would you rather I called back later?"

"No, now's fine. Go right ahead."

"Well," Charley said, "Eugene Barnard just called me and I thought you had better know what he had to say. He and his wife are getting divorced. I suppose that rules him out as president."

"Not necessarily," Prox replied. "It all depends on whether or not there's some scandal about to break. I told him to put chains on his wife or get rid of her. She drinks too much, and I've heard rumors that she's

81

pretty free with her favors. What exactly did Barnard tell you?"

"Not much because I told him not to," Dray said. "I told him that client-attorney conversations were confidential, and that I would feel a conflict of interest if as his lawyer, I learned something I could not share with the other Fellows. He seemed to get that message. He asked whether I could recommend someone else in the firm, but I said I'd rather not. We don't do much divorce work anyhow, and I want to keep several arms lengths away from Barnard until we have chosen a new president."

"I'm sure you made the correct decision," Prox said, "but I wish we knew exactly what was going on. If the wife is shacked up with some man and the word gets out, I'll have to reconsider my support for Gene. Any chance he's misbehaving? If he is, we'll strike him from the list."

"I don't know," Charley said. "I've been Gene's attorney, but I'm not close to either of them, and I'm not on the Yale grapevine. But I'll keep my ears open and let you know what I hear. New Haven's a very small city, or at least my neighborhood is, and that's where the Barnards live."

"You do that," Prox said. "When our committee meets next Saturday, I'll ask you to bring us all up to date." With that, he hung up.

The buzz of conversation had greeted Jerry Walsh as he entered the common room where Arthur Stiles' guests were talking in clusters of twos and threes. Everyone there, Jerry supposed, was deep into gossip about candidates to succeed their host. Picking up a glass of dry vermouth on the rocks, he looked around and decided to wander over to talk to Senator Overman whom he had met only casually. He had just reached her side and introduced himself when Proxmire Young detached himself from Governor Murphy and joined them.

"Are you two deep into a private conversation?" Prox asked. "I need to see you both and this seemed a good moment unless I'm interrupting."

"What's your problem, Prox?" Sis replied. "You rarely have

hesitated to interrupt me in the past." Neither of them noticed as Isabel Doughton approached.

"Come now, dear lady," Prox said. "No one without the courage of a lion dares to halt the flow of your remarks."

"Roar away, master," Sis said. "We were merely exchanging pleasantries, a delight to which we can return when you've completed your mission, whatever it may be."

"Very well," Prox said. "I have reached some tentative conclusions which I want to try on both of you. I'll rely on Jerry to pass them along to the faculty committee. Kindly continue to look casual as I speak, and for now, please keep what I'm saying to yourselves. There's enough noise in here to prevent others from listening in." (Isabel, still unnoticed, smiled.)

"Go ahead, Prox," Jerry said. "What's up?"

Looking around to be sure that no one else was close by, Prox saw Isabel. "Is there something we can do for you?" he asked. Retreating, she shook her head. Prox continued, unaware that she could still hear him. "I'm worried about Barnard. I gather that he and his wife are getting divorced. I also suspect some scandal on her part. I have it on good authority that she sleeps around. I've discussed it with Bishop Manning and he is deeply disturbed. As he says, we just can't have that. If Barnard is going to be smeared, as I expect, he won't do as president. And in any case the bishop and I are dubious about a president without a wife. Look at all Charlotte Stiles does for Yale. Who's to do that if the president isn't married?"

"Lay off, Prox," Jerry said. "I know Gene and Betty very well. They are separating, sure. But she is not a tramp."

"Maybe, maybe not," Prox began when Sis Overman cut in.

"Prox," she said, "why don't you come into the modern world? First of all, Jack Kennedy slept around and that did not prevent him from being a damn good president. The issue is talent, not sex. It's not our business where either of the Barnards sleep so long as they don't flaunt it. Secondly, what makes you think that the next president's spouse is going to be like Charlotte Stiles? Suppose we choose a woman. Do you expect her husband to act as her hostess? Suppose we choose a man whose wife is a physician. Should she have to take charge of the gardens and dinner parties? Grow up, Prox. If Yale thinks the president needs a resident hostess, then let Yale hire a professional hostess to do the job. I'll get you some names if you need them."

"Well, I must say," Prox replied, "I expected a less hostile reception. Contrary to your comments, I will persist in opposing any candidate shrouded with a hint of scandal, though Gene may prove to be free of it, and I will continue to prefer men—yes, Senator, men—married to wives who enjoy helping them and helping Yale." His face ruby-red, Prox spun around and walked away.

At a safe distance, Isabel followed him. What she had heard was juicy but not particularly useful. She thought that soon Proxmire Young would let drop some specific gossip she could retail at a profit. She would have done better eavesdropping on Jerry and Sis Overman.

"My goodness," Sis said as Prox walked away. "I shot to cripple and almost killed. He gets hot when he gets challenged. He was off his feed at our meeting this morning."

"He's certainly hot," Jerry agreed. "Was he going on this way earlier, or shouldn't I ask?"

"No harm in your knowing," Sis said. "He was talking to the committee about candidates. You know, mostly at our meetings he talks. He doesn't much listen. He said that there might be a problem with Barnard, though he didn't expand then. Neither did Bishop Manning. But Prox went on to land on Bob Humber. Said Humber was a hopeless egoist, wouldn't take orders, would ignore the Fellows if he became president. Prox practically said Humber could get the job only over his dead body. Charley objected that others thought highly of Humber, but Prox just brushed Charley aside by asking him, in front of all of us, just how much weight did an alumni Fellow expect to throw around. Prox lost his cool, exactly as he did with us."

At that moment Lilith Furman can up to Jerry and Sis. "You two look pretty intense," Lilith said. "Should I back off?"

"No, no," Jerry said. "We've been talking shop, as you probably guessed."

"Stay put," Sis added. "I'm glad there's another woman here. Prox just dismissed our sex as slaves to their husbands. Jerry and I have been discussing Prox's view about candidates."

"Don't worry," Lilith said. "I'm no candidate."

"Prox thinks I am," Sis said. "He'd hate any woman to be chosen, and I doubt I have any support. The trouble is that he's discarding men so fast that soon no one will be left."

"He was praising one candidate to the skies while he buttonholed me," Lilith said. "Sort of surprised me. I had thought that only I considered Tony Celotto a strong possibility. But Prox came on strong about Tony."

"You've got to watch Prox," Jerry said. "He's nuts about his old secret society. Tony was a member some years after Prox. If Prox is souring on Gene, it's natural for him to pick up Tony."

"Tony's better than you suggest," Lilith objected.

"Okay," Jerry allowed, "but Tony's not a scholar, and we ought to have a scholar."

"I'm less sure than you are," Lilith said, "but I am sure that secret societies don't matter."

"Don't kid yourself," Sis said. "They matter to Prox and the bishop. Fortunately the bishop wasn't in Loaf and Blade, which was the tomb where Prox and Tony bonded. But enough of that. If a scholar is on order, Jerry, what did you think of Aaron Shapiro? I thought he was great."

"I liked everything about him," Jerry said. "Of course you can't learn a great deal in an hour or less of shop talk, but he's obviously a successful researcher, a practiced administrator, and an interesting man. We had no chance to get at his ideas about education except in medicine. I hope we'll see him again. He has the right qualifications if the Fellows are really looking beyond Yale."

"Not quite," Sis said. "He impresses me, too, but while he was raving this morning, Prox made it very clear that he did not want us to consider a Jew. Just like Prox, I'm afraid, but a real obstacle, especially if the bishop and the governor agree. But don't worry, Shapiro's still high on my roster."

"Maybe Prox would relent if Shapiro has a dutiful wife," Lilith suggested.

"Too late," Sis said. "He's a widower."

"Well," Jerry said, putting down his empty glass, "if he proves to be the right guy, maybe we can persuade him to get married again. But first we better have lunch. The others seem to be moving to the tables."

"Ladies and gentlemen," the King said, rising as the luncheon was ending, "thank you for joining me today, and thank you all for all that you have done and are doing for Yale. I hope that this occasion has allowed the members of both committees to get to know each other a little better. And I hope you will join Tony Celotto on a quick inspection of the laboratory at the Medical School where Yale scientists are pursuing landmark research in molecular biology of which Dean Montefiore and I are very proud. Tony and the dean have arranged for a bus, now outside on York Street, to take all of you who are interested to the Sterling Hall of Medicine. After you inspect the lab there, Tony will introduce you to a senior research assistant, and she will take you to the auditorium to show you some slides and explain the significance of the findings. They will surely some day soon have application to medical use on people with diseases like muscular dystrophy. Just now the catalyst in the process, as I understand it, is a powerful poison, but the future will see its benign use. Tony, why don't you lead the way to the bus?"

"What's all this about?" Governor Murphy asked Jerry.

"I don't know," Jerry replied. "You don't have to go if you don't want to."

"I'll pass," Murphy said. I've got to get back to Hartford for the annual Elks' dinner." With that, he departed. Isabel Doughton, disappointed by the absence of exploitable gossip at the luncheon, quietly followed him.

"I'm curious," Lilith said to Jerry. "I'm going to go with Tony. Carter's at home, but he'll wait. How about you?"

"I'm with you," Jerry said. They fell into a fast walk to catch up with Tony and the others.

The visit to the medical school took less than an hour, a few minutes in the lab looking at the elements used, the rest of the time in the auditorium. No one of the Fellows or faculty there except Charlie Lee and Noah Montefiore really understood the explanation offered, but they were all impressed by the potential significance of the experiment. The bus returned them to the main campus shortly before three that afternoon.

"What do you make of that adventure?" Lilith asked Jerry as he was driving her home. "Did the King want to promote science as the appropriate calling for his successor?"

"No, I think not," Jerry replied. "He was expressing his pride and Noah's in what the medical school was accomplishing. He wanted to share that feeling with us. Or so it seems to me."

"You're probably right," Lilith said, "but Noah and Charlie must be delighted that science proved to be the focus of the afternoon."

Jerry Walsh, hoping to arrange a date for a long talk, telephoned Gene Barnard several times that Sunday but no one answered. Both Barnards had had difficult weeks. Gene settled on a lawyer, George Sharpe, a divorce specialist recommended by a colleague. Sharpe had a practice of his own and an office in Hartford, safely remote from New Haven gossip. Gene spent much of Friday with him before driving to Sturbridge, Massachusetts, where he had a weekend rendezvous with Sylvia. She had taken in stride his report about Prox's warning to him. They could find ways to be together, she said, without anyone in New Haven knowing, and she suggested the inn in Sturbridge for a first retreat. She had not said so, but Gene was sure that she was pleased that his divorce was pending. He was delighted by the prospect of their weekend together. He needed to get away from the university and from his own ambitions, he knew, or his nerves would detonate.

Betty, for her part, experienced a great sense of relief that she had at last acted to end her unhappy marriage. She talked at length about the process of divorce with Donna Lazzeri, a Bridgeport lawyer whom she had often used as co-counsel on divorce-related tax problems. With full confidence in Donna, Betty had then put the legal issues out of her mind and turned to her housing problems. After calling several agents, she decided to inspect an apartment in a highrise in Stamford. The highrise promised privacy, especially since she knew no one in that city. And Stamford, as she told herself with a private blush, was an easy drive northeast to Bridgeport to work and southwest to Dobbs Ferry where Aaron lived. She had rented the apartment after inspecting it for just ten minutes, driven at once to a mall near the city where she found a furniture store from which she rented what she knew she needed, and arranged for delivery on Saturday afternoon.

Resolved to start anew, Betty spent Saturday morning at Ricardo's, an expensive hair salon in Greenwich. One of her richest and most chic clients, a local woman who ran a brokerage that netted over a million dollars annually, had recommended the proprietor, a small Italian-American with hands that flew faster than Betty could see. She told him she needed a complete makeover. She wanted to get rid of her French roll, to hide her encroaching gray and recapture the blond hair of her youth, and to replace the severity of her coiffure with something softly curly. "Leave it to me," Ricardo said. Three hours later—she had ordered a facial, too—she emerged from beneath a dryer, looked at herself in a three-way mirror, and smiled in satisfaction. With a brighter lipstick, she thought, she could pass for thirty again.

She bought the lipstick, a bottle of vodka and some groceries, and drank a glass of milk on the way to her new flat where she arrived as the furniture was delivered. Though the apartment's walls were barren and she had as yet no curtains, the place was ready enough to serve as home. She would do more in the coming week, she told herself, but she didn't want to spend the rest of the weekend alone, certainly not after the cosmetic fix she had managed. So she called Aaron Shapiro, not on impulse, she admitted to herself, but because she had been planning to all week. She was too tired for anyone's company that evening, but to her relief, he accepted at once her invitation for Sunday brunch. Time enough to decide whether to prepare it herself after a good night's sleep, she decided, and went to work making her bed and putting the groceries away.

Promptly at ten thirty Sunday, Aaron, who followed the driving directions like a homing pigeon, rang Betty's doorbell. She had just completed her make-up—the new lipstick, some eyeliner, and a dab of Chloe perfume—and she opened the door confident that the crimson sheath she had selected did everything possible for her figure and set off her blond curls. She felt a little like a teenager awaiting a prom date. Aaron entered, handed her a bouquet of fresh flowers, looked her up the down, folded her into his arms, kissed her warmly, stood back, and said, "Wow!"

"The new me," Betty said. "I'm so glad you could make it."

"So am I," Aaron said. "You look wonderful and smell just the same. What have you done to your hair? Whatever it is, you're younger than springtime. The way you look, I'm old enough to be your father."

"I don't need a father, thanks," Betty said. "I just need you."

"And I need you, too," Aaron said, "but first let me take you out to brunch. I had no breakfast and I'm famished."

"I have some English muffins, some eggs, and some bacon," Betty said. "I also have the makings for Bloody Mary's. So if you'll mix the drinks, I'll make brunch and we won't have to go out. Don't worry. I also have three cookbooks. One of them should have directions for poaching eggs."

"No," Aaron said. "If you need a cookbook, you mix the drinks and I'll make brunch. I like to cook, and believe me, after years of being a widower, I've mastered eggs. Maybe later you'll allow me to master you."

"I won't protest," Betty said, hugging him hard. "It's so good to have a man who cares about me in the house. I'd begun to feel like a leper. Freedom is great. I don't want to be married ever again."

"I won't push you," Aaron said as he removed his jacket and headed for the kitchen, "but if you ever change your mind, let me be the first to know."

"I'm not even divorced yet," Betty said. "There's no rush. At least no rush about marriage. And there are things about me that you may not like. I'll remind you, I've been drinking too much since the abortion, and I've staggered into a few beds. Let's not rush. You need to think about what you might be getting into, and so do I."

"I have been thinking," Aaron replied. "I'm prepared to be very patient as long as you don't send me away." She didn't. He left for Dobbs Ferry at a quarter to seven that evening.

That same Sunday Gene Barnard and Sylvia Wheatley awoke in their sunlit room at the Sturbridge Inn, a Massachusetts hostelry not far from Hartford. Curling her arms around Gene, Sylvia kissed him and said, "You know, dear man, I'm a very lucky woman."

"I'm glad you think so," he replied. "I'd say the luck flows the other way."

"Listen to me, I'm serious," Sylvia said. "Seth was never like you. Oh, we loved each other, but there was no passion in it. You make me tingle. As the kids say, you turn me on. And I love it, and I love you."

"I could have said almost the same thing, darling," Gene said. "Let's agree that we're both lucky. And promise me, if you ever think otherwise, or if ever there's something I can do to enhance your happiness, you'll tell me."

"Did you ever know Seth at all?" Sylvia asked. "He was such a thoughtful man, and so clever and artistic. His flower arrangements won prizes from the New Haven Garden Club."

"I remember the flowers," Gene said, "but I knew Seth only casually."

"He and I had a satisfying marriage, nothing like the constant hostility you've told me about between you and Betty, not even any bickering," Sylvia continued. "Seth died much too young, and at first I missed him dreadfully. We had only each other, no children, and I was so lonesome. But after a time I realized that Seth and I had resided together but lived apart. He had his scholarship and I had my children's portraits. We talked about all of that. But we never talked about our real selves. He kept himself hidden, always, totally. And I didn't know the difference until it hit me one night when I couldn't sleep. I decided I'd been lonesome forever."

"But I talk to you," Gene said. "I've told you about my fears and hopes. I've even stopped seeing you every day in order to advance my chances at Yale, and you haven't complained. You're wonderful."

"You telephone me days we are apart," Sylvia replied, "and we talk. You tell me about your day. Seth never did that. Don't ever stop confiding in me. Please don't ever cut me out of any part of your life. I couldn't bear it." She tightened her hold on him and kissed him again, hard.

"Darling," Gene said, "count on me." He meant it. Sylvia had become the pole star in his personal life.

After brunch, they returned to New Haven in their separate cars. As she drove south, Sylvia thought about the weekend just ending. Gene would make a great president of Yale, she was sure. She would never even hint of their relationship until he had the job, and then only after his divorce was final. But it suddenly occurred to her that she'd told Karen Walsh about Gene. She'd remind Karen first chance to say nothing to anyone. While fighting the traffic in Hartford, Sylvia sighed. She would miss seeing Gene except on weekends away, but at least he'd call every evening. She must remain an intimate part of his life.

Robert Humber, encouraged by Archie Mound, decided that a good offense made the best defense. So that Sunday evening, in a state of obvious agitation, he called Charley Dray. "I don't like intruding on your leisure," Humber said, "but I have to talk to you. I want to change signals. I've decided that I want to be an announced candidate for the presidency. I'm going to report my decision to the *Yale Daily News* and through that channel to the wire services. That will build alumni support for me. I wanted to tell you first because you've been so forthright with me."

"Slow down, Bob," Charley replied. "Prox is no fan of yours and he won't like your going public. It will give him another reason for opposing you."

"To hell with Proxmire Young," Humber said. "The letters for me will overwhelm him."

"I'm not so sure," Charley said. "I don't like your plan myself. The search is not a public matter, and we intend to keep it that way. I beg you to think it over."

"I have thought it over. Your committee is dawdling. What were you doing following the King down to the medical school yesterday? Yale can't afford to have some goddamn scientist as president. The university needs someone who will create a whole new environment, requirements in Yale College that will make students face their heritage and alert them to the nonsense of women's studies or black studies or Jewish studies. I'm the only one around with the guts to stand up and fight for western values. I'm the only one who will use the platform of the presidency to attack the liberal crap that's destroying the country. I'm the only one in the whole university that won't buy the Supreme Court's idiotic decisions about school prayer and abortion. Yale needs me, and the alumni are going to demand my appointment."

"Bob, you're raving." Charley said. "Frankly I agree with much of what you say, but you're going about it the wrong way. If you don't back off, Prox will crucify you."

"Let him try, pal," Humber said. "I've plenty of friends who will warn him that they will give no more money to Yale unless the place changes its ways. I called to tell you, not to ask your advice. You go ahead and tell Young if you want to. Neither you nor he is going to deter me."

The phone clicked as Humber hung up. "Damn all," Charley said to himself. "He's out of his mind, but he can cause a lot of trouble." That was exactly what he told Prox Young whom he called at once to inform him about Humber's decision.

"I don't understand why Humber thinks he can operate that way," Prox said. "I'm going to let him hang himself, and I urge you to do the same. But I don't know what's got into him."

They learned more the next day. Monday's *Yale Daily* carried a story that also ran in most east coast papers. Humber had not just announced his candidacy. He had also denounced what he called "the surrender of the academy to liberalism, the first cousin of communism." He had attacked the Supreme Court, affirmative action programs, and legalized abortion. And he had pledged himself to lead a conservative crusade "to restore Christian values to Yale and the nation."

No one was more stunned than Arthur Stiles who telephoned Prox Young right after reading the *Times* at breakfast. "I know, I know," Prox said as soon as he heard the King's voice. "I hope you agree that the best policy is to ignore Humber's blast."

"Of course," the King said, "but what provoked it?"

"I don't know," Prox answered. "Charles Dray thinks it may have been your excursion to the Medical School. Humber seems to have a grudge against science. Whatever his problem, you can count on me to bury him."

"He's a very stubborn man," the King said. "He'll not give up his ambitions lightly. At best, the Yale corporation is in for a flood of nasty mail. So be prepared. I'll get some mail, too, and I'll let you know if any of it is important. Let's keep in touch."

ISABEL

Isabel interpreted Robert Humber's tactic through her own special lenses. He was determined, she believed, to send her no money. Thus the agitation he had stirred up. If she now reported his sick sexual tastes to Proxmire Young, Humber would deny her accusations and attribute them to an attack by his liberal enemies. He'd probably get away with it. She would need more time to find or contrive something so damaging that he could not ignore even the threat to disclose it.

Meanwhile, she needed funds to replenish her bank account. Unfortunately she had found nothing sufficiently incriminating about the Barnards to permit her successfully to hit on the professor. So she would have to do what she could with her informed hunch about Tony Celotto. She did not like to pick on her boss who was always decent to her. But she knew he wanted to be president and she suspected he was vulnerable.

Isabel had overhead gossip in Mama Celotto's grocery store that suggested Mama was hiding something about Tony or about the family's immigration to the United States from Amalfi. An elderly Italian-American woman, unaware that Isabel understood her native language, had told Mama in Italian within Isabel's hearing to stop worrying about the Immigration and Naturalization Service. The INS, the woman went on, had been told by the congresswoman from New Haven to leave the Celotto son alone. His mother was a useful member of the congresswoman's district.

Isabel reckoned that Tony was too young to have come to America in the 1930s with his parents. Further, she recalled from conversations of her father's that Mama alone had made a long trip to Italy about 1947, about the time Tony would have been born. Isabel also knew from local gossip that the Celottos had been classified as enemy aliens during World War II. Only after her husband died had Mama Celotto become a naturalized citizen. Until then she had humored his fantasy of one day returning to Amalfi to stay. On the basis of that information, Isabel surmised that Tony had been born in Italy while his mother was there, born of Italian parents. Some simple research lent credibility to Isabel's hunch. The Celottos had resided in New Haven since their arrival in the United States but the city's records contained no birth certificate for Tony. It looked to Isabel as if he was not an American citizen. Perhaps he was even subject to deportation, but she knew too little law to be sure.

Surmise in itself provided less than a solid basis for trying to extract money from Tony. But Isabel felt confident that Mama Celotto, whose pride in Tony lighted her life, would pay plenty to avoid any suspicion about her son, especially while he was hoping to become president of Yale. If Isabel's surmise was correct, if Tony was an illegal alien, Mama would be scared to death. So Isabel leaned on Mama. After swallowing her disappointment over Robert Humber's resistance, she turned to her computer and tried several drafts of a note to Mama. She settled on her fourth effort:

This is a warning! How would you like it if I told the Yale Daily News the facts about Tony's birth? I know all about it. I'll keep quiet for a price, which I expect you to pay as soon as I write you again. Until then, say nothing. If you're tempted to discuss this note with anyone, you had better think first about Tony and his father.
Snoopy

7.
DECISION

The brouhaha over Humber remained in the news for a few days and then faded. During the week the Yale president's office and the Yale alumni magazine received between them some thirty-seven letters, mostly critical of Humber, though the letters in his support were longer and angrier. Archie Mound, football hero and alumni Fellow, announced that he would vote for Humber for president. Jerry Walsh told Lilith Furman that Archie had taken too many blows to the head. But Prox Young found both the publicity and the mail upsetting, and he knew Mound would make a fuss as long as Humber wanted him to. Determined to accelerate the selection process before more trouble erupted, Prox made sure that all members of the search committee would be at the Century Association for the scheduled Saturday meeting.

The Thursday before the group assembled, Prox made a special trip to New Haven to see Tony Celotto. He arrived at the Yale campus at eleven that morning. Telling his driver to wait for him on Wall Street to the side of Woodbridge Hall, Prox walked into the building, went through the front room in Tony's suite, past Isabel Doughton who looked at him in astonishment, and into Tony's office without knocking. He closed the door behind him, shook Tony's hand, and sat down facing Tony's desk. No longer surprised by anything Prox did, Tony grinned at him and said, "Prox, you had better be careful. If you continue to do what you just did, Miss Doughton will drop dead of a heart attack. She's supposed to guard my privacy, and she takes her job seriously."

"She'll die of a heart attack anyway because she's too fat," Prox replied. "I've no time to waste on her. I have to tell you two things. First, I want you to stop acting as secretary of our search committee. As far as I'm concerned, you're now one of the leading candidates for the presidency, and I don't want your presence at the meetings to inhibit discussion. Now don't say anything until I finish. I must get back to Manhattan as soon as I can. Secondly, I want you to think about university problems and what you'd do about them. That way you'll be prepared when the Fellows interview you. And right now you have five minutes to think about anything in your private life that might disqualify you for the presidency. I want to know about it before I tell the others you have my blessing. You do, too, unless you're in the middle of some secret affair, or guilty of embezzlement, or some such."

"Prox," Tony said, "you know me better than that. I have no secrets, never have had. But as it happens, my parents adopted me. My father's sister, my actual mother, died when I was born in New York. Her husband, my actual father, was much older than she, so with his encouragement my legal parents adopted me. And they have been wonderful. Frankly, I've not dared to believe that I'm a serious candidate for the presidency, but of course I'd love it. I'm proud to have your confidence, but, remember, I have no Ph.D. And my parents were born in Italy."

"I don't care about your adoption or the origins of your parents," Prox said. "I didn't know your father but I think your mother's great. Don't worry about the Ph.D. Barnard has one and he's screwed up his life anyway. We can't have a messy divorce hanging over us with one Fellow already out in public for that nut, Humber. I need you, Tony. I need a horse of my own to beat Mound's horse. And I intend mine to be a Yale man, a qualification that Dray and the bishop also prefer. So stay loose, boy. I'm going to speed things along. Barnard and Humber can have their claques. My guy is going to get the gold ring."

Prox was rising to his feet as he finished. He started for the door, stopped to ask Tony to call his office and say he'd be there in two hours, and strode out. If as he left he had looked at Isabel Doughton, who had been eavesdropping, he would have seen the shocked chagrin on her face.

Prox was still manic on Saturday at the Century. At the outset of the meeting, he told the others that Tony would no longer attend their sessions. "He's a leading candidate," Prox said, "and I don't want him here while we talk. Let's get moving right away to agree on a short list for the faculty committee to review. We've got to settle the issue before Humber and his fans stir things up further. Let's get right to it."

"That's agreeable as far as I'm concerned," Bishop Manning said. "I would like, however, to keep Gene Barnard in mind. We don't really know that he's involved in any scandal. Until I'm better informed about him, he remains my preference."

"Have it your way for now," Prox said. "Barnard is no problem on a short list. We still have time to look into his recent behavior. But I still am dubious about an unmarried president."

"How about a widower?" Sis Overman asked. "I want us to meet with Shapiro again. He seems ideal to me, but his wife died some time ago."

"Then I have reservations about him, too," Prox said. "And I'm still uneasy about a Jew. But I see no harm in having his name on the short list."

"I'm sure you're uneasy about women, too," Sis said.

"Have we one in mind?" Prox asked.

"I do," Charley Dray said. "Sis is going to be on my short list. I can't support Humber any longer, and I share your feelings about Barnard and Shapiro, at least for the time being. Further, I have a special regard for the cerebral processes of lawyers. And Sis's judgments have impressed me. Don't blush, Sis, and you can stay right here because we're not going to talk about you any more today."

"Thank you, Charley," Sis said, "for protecting womanhood. I'll have to brood some more about whether I'm available."

"Just a minute," Prox said. "Didn't we agree to exclude ourselves and anyone who is not in the academy? Two strikes on Sis."

"That was then," Charley said. "This is now."

"Haven't we just about constructed a short list?" Governor Murphy asked. "We should put Humber on it so that we can say we did. That may appease people like Mound."

"Thank God there aren't many people like Mound," Sis said. "But I think you're right. How about it, Prox?"

"Let's see," Prox said. "What we seem to have, if I can read my own notes, is Barnard, Celotto, Humber, and Shapiro. And I'll put Overman down, too, Charley, to keep you happy. Is that right? If so, let's give the list to Jerry Walsh as soon as we can. Then he should be able to get his committee to meet some evening next week and get back to us before next Saturday. Meanwhile we can break up into two groups, if you're willing, and one group can spend some time with Barnard and Shapiro, the other with Celotto. We don't really need to see Sis, do we, or to interview Humber?"

"The Celotto group should talk shop with Sis," Dray said. "I'm serious about her even if you aren't, Prox. We need to know what Sis considers her priorities for Yale."

"Okay, Charley," Prox said. "You and Peter interview Sis and Celotto, and I guess you better at least go through the motions with Humber. I will join Sis and the governor in the other group."

"No can do," Governor Murphy said. "The legislature is in special session briefly next week. I have to nurse my budget for extraordinary expenses through on Wednesday and Thursday. I'll need all Monday and Tuesday to prepare, and Friday to pick up the pieces. But I want to say something else before the rest of you go off. I'm content with the list. But I want you to be dead serious when you talk to Humber. I know he's acted up. But I still respect him. His piece in *Commentary* last spring on eliminating the income tax made excellent sense. He'd be a fresh breeze at Yale. Don't write him off yet. He's been angry. He's very, very good when he's in harness. And we know he'd take the job."

"Not my view," Prox said, "but I promise we'll hear him out. Now I guess we can all go home, unless there's something else." There was nothing else that morning.

"Never has he said anything interesting about education, at least not in my hearing. He's a charmer, I admit, but just how is he qualified to be president of Yale?" Roger Gordon slapped the table for emphasis. He was expounding that view at the meeting of the faculty search committee in Jerry Walsh's office the Wednesday evening after Proxmire Young had given Jerry the short list. The discussion had begun with Roger's opposition to Gene Barnard.

"Hey, I thought you and Gene were pals," Jerry said.

"We are, sort of," Rog allowed. "We play a lot of squash and tennis together, but we're not close otherwise. Mind you, I like Gene. Who doesn't? But liking is not enough. As I see it, Gene's not even much of a scholar. Just that first, popular book."

"You're pretty damn critical," Jerry replied, "but at least we know where you stand."

"As a matter of fact," Charlie Lee said, "I agree with Roger. Barnard might do as dean of the college, but he would flunk as president. Not strong enough. No convictions, just expedients. Except for you, Jerry, who does intend to vote for Barnard? Or for Senator Overman? We've already decided, no public people. She's no scholar. She doesn't know science. We've been over all that."

"That's right," Lilith said. "We don't have to cover old ground again, and these chairs we're sitting on are murder. Where did you get them, Jerry? Or do you want chairs like this to keep the students from lingering?"

"They're from the seminar room across the hall," Jerry told her. "Go on over and sit next to Noah on the couch. We still have work to do."

"Maybe not much," Noah Montefiore said, moving over to make room for Lilith's ample seat. "Lilith is correct, Jerry. And so is Roger. I doubt if anyone but you thinks enough of Gene to want him as president. No substance. Sure, he can talk the birds off the trees, and he's an Old Blue who titillates the alums. Maybe he should become some kind of roving money raiser. But let's get on to the others unless there's more to say about Gene."

"I remain Gene's fan," Jerry said. "I'm prepared to go on, and Charlie said all we need to hear about Senator Overman, I think. Anyone disagree?"

"Somewhat," Lilith said. "She's very quick and her judgment as a lawyer has always been excellent, but I'm willing to abide by our earlier decision about public figures."

"We needn't linger over Robert Humber, I should think," Noah said. "His behavior strikes me as having been reprehensible. And I wholly disagree with all he stands for. I can't understand why he's still on the Fellows' list."

"I'll second that," Roger said.

"I'll bet he's on that list just to keep Mr. Mound shut up," Jerry said. "I agree with Noah, Humber may have the best mind of them all, but he's a terror when he makes it up."

"Look where we are," Roger Gordon said. "Most of us don't want Barnard. No one is for Humber or Overman, as far as I can see. That leaves Celotto and Shapiro."

"A scientist of standing is exactly what Yale needs," Noah said emphatically.

"Hear, hear," Roger added.

"When we met with Shapiro, I must say he impressed me," Jerry said. "We should nevertheless talk about Tony a little. Everyone likes Tony, but he lacks a Ph.D. and he's never been a faculty member."

"He has some assets," Lilith said. "He runs a tight ship. He's a star in relations with the town. He knows a great deal about academic administration. And the alumni love him."

"I repeat," Roger said, "love is not enough. I'm looking for scholarship as well as leadership. I want a proven educator, not an alumni icon. I like Tony, too. I certainly prefer him to Humber. I also prefer him to Barnard because I believe Gene is shallow, and I can't tell about Tony because I don't know him as well. But Shapiro will get my vote. He has it all."

"If Proxmire Young will swallow a Jew," Jerry said. "That seems unlikely to me."

"Another reason to support Shapiro," Lilith said. "If he's our favorite, we'll put the finger on Mr. Young. He'll feel the pressure, maybe relent."

"Don't count on that," Jerry said. "Prox has his own internal gyro. He'll hold out if he's in a mood to."

"He said he wanted our advice," said Charlie Lee. "We'll tell him Shapiro. That's the end of our responsibility. We do not worry about Mr. Young's prejudices."

"Just one thing," Lilith said. "When you see Young, Jerry, do you have to tell him about our deliberations, or can you just tell him about our vote, once we've taken it?"

"I think we should work out a priority list of our own and have Jerry give him that," Rog said.

"Yes," Noah said. "Tell him Overman and Humber are unacceptable, and list the others in order of the vote."

"Are you all agreeable to that?" Jerry asked. They all nodded.

"O.K.," Jerry said, passing around sheets of typing paper. "Unless someone objects, let's vote. Why not first list only your first choice and those who you find unacceptable. Then we'll see what we have and go on from there." Again there were nods all around.

Jerry opened the folded sheets he received one by one and examined them carefully. "Lilith can check my count after I tell you that all but one ballot listed Humber as out, and all but one listed Overman as out. Shall we make that unanimous?" They all agreed to.

"Now as to the first choices," Jerry said, handing the papers to Lilith to check. "One for Barnard. One for Celotto. Three for Shapiro."

"Let's report it just that way," Roger suggested. "No one will miss that Shapiro has a majority. I don't object to the Fellows knowing the other two had some support."

"Agreed?" Jerry asked. "If so, we can adjourn, but let's be damned sure no one leaks a word. If there are going to be any leaks, I don't want them coming from the faculty. Let the Fellows discipline themselves. I'll call Prox tomorrow."

"Shouldn't you also tell King Arthur confidentially?" Roger asked. "He deserves to know where we stand."

"Good idea," Noah said, and the others murmured assent.

"Will do," Jerry said. "Thanks, you all have been great. Let's hope we're really at the end of the line. Lilith, come on and I'll drive you home." As they reached his car, he added, "This is going to be a shock for Prox."

"He'll survive," Lilith said. "It's past time he learned that his hangups aren't universal."

Proxmire Young was determined to keep the proceedings of his search committee confidential, especially as they moved toward a decision. He arranged therefore to join Sis Overman in Washington where, with little chance of being observed by curious Yale faculty or students, they could talk privately at whatever length they liked with Gene Barnard and Aaron Shapiro. The very Wednesday that Jerry's group met, Prox and Sis had scheduled luncheon with Barnard and dinner with Shapiro.

A few minutes before noon Sis met Prox at the private suite he had booked in the Mayflower Hotel. Her Connecticut Avenue office was only a walking distance away. Prox offered her a drink when she arrived, and after a pause, she asked for bourbon and branch. "I hesitated," Sis said, "because I want to be cold sober when I raise hell, as I am about to. I have absolutely no intention of becoming president of any university. I have allowed others to use my name only because I was resolved to press you on the matter of women. You have been unspeakably awful to try to exclude women from consideration. Because I failed to find a woman candidate whom I could support with enthusiasm, I thought it worth letting my name go forward in order to test your tolerance and perhaps to expand your narrow horizons. But that game has to end before it becomes embarrassing. So I'm telling you now that there is no need for anyone to interview me about higher education. I am not a candidate. But I also despise your narrow-mindedness. I warn you now, I shall raise a public stink about your attitude toward women unless you shape up and get rid of your prejudiced opposition to Jews and to men or women who have had the misfortune to need a divorce to escape a marriage gone sour. You and I have two important interviews today. If you do not take those men with utter seriousness, without regard for their private lives or personal ancestry, I swear to you, I'll cut you and Yale, too, to pieces in a statement to the newspapers tomorrow."

"I am not accustomed to rudeness," Prox replied, his face crimson, his pulse racing. "But I can give as well as I can take. I've always found you a self-righteous pain. You have no grounds for questioning my judgments or my reasons for making them. Disagree if you like, but do not suppose you understand my motives. I am concerned in this search only with what's good for Yale. I happen to believe, along with many others, that a Jew will be disadvantaged in raising money from the alumni. So, too, a woman or a man tainted by personal scandal. And I consider a loyal wife a major asset for a president. There are many things about me you don't know. My older daughter is married to a Jew, and their marriage had my blessing. He's a good man and a very good investment banker who's now a senior vice president in my firm. Incidentally, he agrees with me about Yale, though he attended Ohio State. I know all about nasty divorces. My parents had one. It shook my father who was never again the same. And the scandal was all my mother's making. So I have not been persecuting you or Shapiro or Barnard's wife. I have been thinking about Yale and its future."

"All right, Prox," Sis said. "You have had, you believe, reasons to be prejudiced, but that does not alter the prejudice. Frankly, I meant to offend you. I think I may hate you. I see no need to withdraw or repeat what I've already said. But I'll admit to your concern about Yale, and if that concern is genuine, you should support the ablest candidate without regard to his religion or marriage. I'll keep my mouth shut if it is that kind of concern and not some dumb bias that determines your assessment of our guests today. I think we can get along together on that basis."

"Good," Prox replied, "at least we can try. Save your passion for another time. Now I need a drink, and I expect Gene Barnard will be here any minute." As he poured himself some single malt Scotch whiskey, the desk phoned to say that a Mr. Barnard was there. "Send him up," Prox said. Turning to Sis he added, "make sure you ask him about the divorce. I'll listen and compare notes later. I'll start him on other matters."

"And I realize that the budget may not permit any new faculty hiring. So Yale will have to be especially careful about replacing those who resign or retire. That may call for some modifications in appointment procedures, though I haven't thought through what changes may be desirable." With those words Gene Barnard finished his description of the changes he believed necessary in the management of Yale. He was replying to Prox Young's questions. Gene felt pretty good about himself and his statement. After all, he had been through the interview with Prox before, and Prox had told him essentially to repeat to the Fellows what he had then said to Prox. Now he had done so in the presence of Senator Overman who had explained that she and Prox were representing the Corporation's search committee. Gene looked at her to try to measure her response.

"Professor Barnard," Sis said, her face expressionless, "I have a couple of further questions, if you don't mind. First, do you want to be the next president of Yale, and if so, what makes you think you're qualified to be?"

"Oh, yes, I would like very much to be the president of Yale," Gene said. "It has been my ambition for a long time. I am a Yale man. The place lies next to my heart, indeed it has done so since my freshman year. I really believe in the last words of the alma mater, 'for God, for country and for Yale.' Only in my case Yale comes first. Just please give me the chance and I'll be a great president. Like Arthur Stiles, whom I've studied for years. Only different and better, more attuned to the alumni, more cooperative with the Fellows, less buddy-buddy with the undergraduates."

"I hear you," Sis replied, "but I want you to know that I have the highest opinion of President Stiles, and I think his priorities have been just right. Now what are your special assets for the post?"

"Well," Gene said," as I say, I've been studying the job. I've also served on many responsible committees. I was chairman of the Humanities Divisional Committee for three years. I'm now a member of the divisional committee on the biological sciences. I know the college faculty, most of its tenured members by name. I know their views about appointments and the curriculum, and I've just told you what I think about those things. I've been one of the most popular lecturers at Yale for about ten years. I've written a best seller about the Roman emperors and won a Pulitzer for it. Most people who know me seem to like me. And I think I'm ready to take over."

"Thank you," Sis said, still with a poker face. "Now I must ask you one more question. There are those on the Corporation worried about possible scandal in connection with your divorce. Can you reassure me about that? And how do you plan to manage without a wife as your official hostess?"

Gene reflected before answering. Prox had more or less warned him that the divorce might matter, so he had a reply ready. But he wondered if either Prox or the senator had some suspicion about him and another woman. What rumors might they have heard? He did not dare to bring Sylvia into the conversation until the divorce was final, some time after the Fellows had made their decision. So he would have to be careful now.

"Ours is an uncontested divorce," he replied. "Neither my wife nor I is accusing the other of any breach of faith. We simply do not get along any more. That kind of incompatibility has become pretty common in our times. That's why the divorce laws are liberal. We have no disagreements about property either. Neither of us is going to make a fuss. So I can think of no basis for scandal, and I foresee none. As to a hostess if I become president, for a while I would have to employ a social secretary, which is, as I realize, a less than ideal arrangement. But some day I may marry again, and then the problem will solve itself."

"Are you so sure that a wife will want to play the role of hostess?

Today's women have careers of their own," Sis said.

Damn, Gene thought to himself, I've offended her feminist sensibilities. Aloud he said, "The kind of woman with whom I'm likely to fall in love will be glad to work with me, I'm sure."

"For your sake and particularly for hers," Sis said, "I hope you're right."

"Gene, thank you," Prox said, eager to end the interview before Sis galloped off into her sisterhood persona. "You were good to come all the way to Washington for this luncheon. I'm glad you understood our need for confidentiality. Please say nothing to anyone about our chat. Incidentally, Jerry Walsh and his committee do know you're on our list. No need for them to know more now. We hope to have a decision in a week or two. Meanwhile, good luck. I expect to see you in New Haven before we're much older."

"Thank you, Prox, and you, Senator Overman," Gene said. "As I've said, I hope to see you both regularly in the future at Fellows' meetings. I see I didn't eat much. Too busy talking I guess. But thanks for lunch. I'll let myself out and run for the next shuttle to New York."

"He makes a good impression," Prox said as the door closed behind Gene.

"On you," Sis said. "I find him banal. He'd be a great come down from Arthur Stiles. He has nothing new to offer, Prox, just more of the same with a prudent and self-serving regard for the Fellows. Maybe unobjectionable but also uninspired. He wants the job, but we must do better than that. And I sure hope the woman he finds is an old-fashioned lassie. He's stuck up on himself, Prox. He lives in yesterdays' world. I bet he doesn't get much support on the faculty committee."

"I'll bet you're wrong. I found him sound about education, and I'm relieved by what he said about his divorce. He'll be high on my list," Prox said. "You've just got one of your feminist mads on. I was afraid of that when he talked about a next wife."

"We'll each report to the committee," Sis said, "or so I assume. So there's no point in our battling here. I'd like to go back to my office after I finish my coffee. I should return by six this evening, right? I'll ask Shapiro about his idea of who is to be hostess. I'll wager he makes more sense than Gene did."

"We'll see," Prox replied. "I hope you come back in a better mood, though sweet, simple and girlish would be too much to expect. Until six, then."

They were finishing coffee and dessert, a fresh fruit cup with lemon sherbet. They had been at the table, a portable table Prox had ordered for their dinner, for over two hours. "That's very interesting, Dr. Shapiro," Proxmire Young said. "If Yale were to join the city in expanding and endowing Science Park, faculty in the sciences could work with entrepreneurs who rented there. We'd have to figure out a policy for released time and for the university's reimbursement, but as you say, Viney Medical University could provide a useful model. And Yale could use the income, as well as the available facilities. Clever of you to have done something like that in Yonkers. But we should let you go. You have a plane to catch. Any other questions, Senator?"

"I've two," Sis Overman said. "I know this sounds intrusive, Dr. Shapiro, but some of the Fellows are worried about how you'd manage without a wife as your hostess."

"Not very well, Senator," Shapiro said. "I suppose I could hire a professional hostess when I had to, but I'd much rather have a wife, and confidentially, I hope I soon will."

"That's wonderful," Sis said. "I'm happy for you both. My other question you may have expected. If you're asked to be the president of Yale, will you accept the offer? Some of my male colleagues have exposed egos, at least as far as the university is concerned, and they hate to be rejected."

"I would not have joined you tonight if I had no interest in the Yale presidency," Shapiro said. "Of course I'd have to consider the exact terms of any offer, and I can't do more now than to say that I expect I would find them to my taste."

"Fair enough," Sis said. "Many thanks for coming so far on such a busy day."

"Yes, many thanks," Prox added. "I've much enjoyed the evening, and I've learned a great deal. We'll be in touch within a fortnight, I hope. Have you any questions before you go?"

"None at all," Shapiro replied. "You've answered every question I had in mind. Thanks to you both, and good night. I'll run to try to make the next shuttle to LaGuardia." He picked up his topcoat and strode to the door.

"There goes a good man," Sis said as the door closed. "And sexy as hell. I was bowled over again."

"I can't measure his sex appeal, but I have to agree that he's impressive," Prox said, nodding his head. "And about to acquire a wife, which is also good. I guarantee I'll take him very seriously and tell the others so when we all meet."

"That's all I can ask," Sis said. "What he said about computers and miniaturization fascinated me. I'd never thought until I heard him that soon we may all have computers the size of a wallet. He's thought that through in terms of higher education, too. Just think of every student having a computer in her pocket."

"Stay put, Sis, and have a brandy with me," Prox suggested. "You have no plane to make, and I'd like to chat informally, no agenda, to show you that I'm not as demonic as you suppose. We got off on the wrong foot years ago at that senate hearing."

"I'd almost forgotten that, Prox," Sis replied. "Did I scare your investor's pants off? I was putting on a populist show in which I half believed. Still do. But you were on your very best behavior tonight. I'd like to stay, but I've an early morning meeting and a tough day ahead. So I'm out of here, thank you anyway."

"Then go along," Prox said, pouring himself a large snifter. "Thanks for all your help. I'll see you next Saturday in New Haven. I'll be curious to learn what Peter and Charley have to say about Humber and Celotto. I like Tony, but I doubt he will measure up to today's visitors."

"I doubt any of the others will measure up to Dr. Shapiro," Sis said. She surprised herself and Prox by kissing him on the forehead. "Good night, Prox. Sleep well. You've earned it."

For Proxmire Young, the meeting of the search committee on the following Saturday, the last Saturday that October, came as an anticlimax. He had already made up his mind and counted the votes he needed. But he went through the motions of deliberation with scrupulous care. Governor Murphy had political commitments that detained him but he told Prox to cast his vote for him. "I would agree with you in the end in any case," Murphy added. So only four of the group assembled at the corporation table, with Prox sitting at the west end, Sis on his right, and Bishop Manning and Charley Dray next to each other on his left.

"Sis and I have seen Barnard and Shapiro, and we'll fill you in after you report your impressions of Celotto and Humber," Prox began.

"There's not much that's positive to report," Bishop Manning said. "Humber was impossible. He said he was far and away the best man for the presidency, but he did not expect us to elect him. None of us except Mound had the right stuff in him. He and Mound would write a circular letter to all alumni after we fell on our collective faces. I had the distinct feeling that he would be disappointed if he were chosen. What he really wants is a fight."

"I wholly agree," Charley said. "Just write him off."

"Tony Celotto, in contrast, is the salt of the earth," the bishop continued. "He's also totally ingenuous. He told us that he had never considered himself a serious candidate until you spoke to him, Prox. He said he'd love the job but had not reached many conclusions about future policy. Essentially he proposed to rely on faculty members he liked and trusted, one to become provost, though he named no names, others to head up the divisional committees and the course of study committee, still others to replace deans as they retired. He thought Professor Walsh might do well as dean of the graduate school, and he said he wanted to find a visible spot for Lilith Furman, who's a special friend. He's for more women in administration. His appointees would know what needed doing, he said, and he'd follow their leads. I came away convinced Tony would make a great headmaster at Choate but

110

that Yale was too much for him. And of course he's light on the usual credentials."

"Alas, I agree again," Charley said. "He's a lovely guy, but not for 43 Hillhouse."

"Sis," Prox asked, "do you mind if I begin for us?"

"Not in the least," Sis replied.

"Well, gentlemen," Prox said, "I cannot tell you how grateful I am to our own senator. Sis has made quite an impression on me this week. First she scolded me for my prejudices, and when I thought it over, I concluded she was right. I had liked to believe that I had only the good of Yale in mind. Sis reminded me that prejudice is prejudice whatever the excuse. And it occurred to me that if I could support Tony, who's a Catholic, I could support Shapiro unless I was anti-Semitic. I did not like to think of myself or of Yale that way. More important, Shapiro made both of us sit up and take notice, and not for the first time, though I had previously resisted saying so. Wednesday evening he was full of splendid ideas about possible income from science, about the future of computers in higher education, about ways to make introductory science and math courses more palatable to resistant undergraduates, about the need for more high level administrators at Yale, and on and on. While he was still talking I found myself convinced he was our man, though Gene Barnard has lots on his side, too. But, as Sis said after we talked to Gene, he was banal. Especially compared to Shapiro. Further, I learned the next day that the faculty committee had a clear majority for Shapiro. So I bow to Sis, to Jerry Walsh's gang, and to my new ability to see the light. I'm for Shapiro. How about you, Sis?"

"I'm breathless," Sis said. "I could kiss you if I hadn't already done so the other evening. Prox, dear man, as Theodore Roosevelt once said, 'It is not having been in the dark house that matters, it is having come out.' Of course I agree with you."

"Seems to me," Charley said, "that that settles it. You have the governor's vote, Prox, and Sis is with you, and now, after this whole exercise, so am I."

"You may take that as unanimous," the bishop said, "and properly ecumenical. I'm so glad we all agree, and relieved, too, that it's all over."

"Not yet over," Prox said. "We need still to take our recommendation to the other Fellows at the regular meeting a week hence. They can accept or reject it as they choose, though with your help, I'll make a strong case. Then if they agree, we have to ask Shapiro officially. He seemed ready to say yes, but we'll have to give him the details of an offer. Meanwhile we must keep our recommendation absolutely secret. Agreed?"

"Naturally," said Sis, "but in strict confidence can't you tell the King where we stand?

"Will do," Prox said. "As we adjourn, we should congratulate ourselves, and Yale, too, on our good sense."

ISABEL

A sense of frustration just about overwhelmed Isabel. Humber, she had to admit, had long since refused to serve as a source of funds. Mama Celotto had proved to be beyond her reach. The gossip Isabel had collected about the Barnards remained too vague to be useful. And Tony had no more minutes for her to transcribe. Isabel had resumed her late-night walks, binoculars in hand, but as yet to no avail, and the nights were becoming uncomfortably colder. She found herself eating more and more chocolate candy.

BOOK TWO

THE COLLAR AND
THE CORPSE

8.
SURPRISES

On a gray, wet November Saturday they arrived in ones and twos, entered Woodbridge Hall, and climbed the handsome stairway to the second floor. There they deposited their damp coats in the president's office to the right and then doubled back and walked across the hall to the corporation room. The fifteen men and women of the Yale Corporation were meeting to elect a new president of the university. As they took their seats, Isabel Doughton, on extra duty again—and all ears—served those who wanted it a cup of coffee. It was weak, Sis Overman thought to herself, but she was grateful for the warmth. She looked around the room. Each Fellow had a brass nameplate fixed to his or her designated chair. All the Fellows' chairs were filled except for Proxmire Young's who had yet to appear. As Sis finished her coffee, he arrived, went round the table to shake hands with everyone, sat down not in his chair but in the president's, and opened the meeting with a brief review of the search and a succinct description of Aaron Shapiro and his qualifications. It was a redundant exercise since he had talked to them all by phone during the week.

"Does anyone from the search committee want to add a word or two?" Prox asked.

"Just an 'amen' to what you have said," Bishop Manning replied. "I think we've reached a most fortunate decision, and I hope you will all vote to make it unanimous."

"Not a chance," Archie Mound snarled. "I've seen this coming, and

I'm against it. I don't know why in the name of the Lord you have had the unmitigated gall to nominate an outsider when all along an outstanding Yale man, no, the outstanding Yale man has been available and wants the job. What's more, he alone of the candidates I'm told you have considered stands for the values that have made this place great. You all know damned well that I'm referring to Dean Robert Humber of the Law School. You are not going to get me to support some doctor named Shapiro. And if you elect him, I'll organize every donor who has given Yale more than ten thousand dollars in the last decade to go on strike."

"I'm sure you'll try, Archie," Prox said. "Now, if no one has anything else to offer, I move we vote."

"Second," Bishop Manning said.

"I insist on a secret ballot," Mound said.

"Of course," Prox said. "I have paper and envelopes ready. Will you agree to open and count them with Senator Overman?"

"Absolutely not," Mound said. "I've decided instead to resign, effective immediately. I'm fed up with the Proxmire Young steamroller. You are all going to regret this." He pushed back his chair, rose, slammed the table with both hands, and hurried out.

"Let's not worry about Archie," Charley Dray said. "He was born with a silver thorn in his mouth."

"Ready everyone?" Prox asked, and he passed around the ballots. Senator Overman stood up, moved behind his chair, opened the envelopes as they were returned to his place, read their contents, and announced that the vote was unanimous.

"That does it," Prox said, "except for a formal acceptance. I'll try to reach Dr. Shapiro after I review the terms of the offer with the prudential committee, and we'll do that after we finish our regular business. Until he has agreed to serve, please no leaks. Now let's tell King Arthur and the other officers that we're ready to begin the regular meeting."

Archie Mound, pursuing the plan he had made with Bob Humber, quickly reached Humber's office in the law school where they had stored the envelopes they had already stamped and addressed to the alumni Mound had just identified before his resignation. Those letters, which they mailed at the Church Street post office ten minutes later, contained the request they had signed jointly to wealthy alumni to punish Yale "for the persistent and irresponsible liberalism of the President and Fellows" by withholding contributions to the university until Proxmire Young was replaced by Mound "or some other spokesman for the long-neglected principles of the civilization of the Christian West."

Humber and Mound had also prepared a press release quoting their letter as part of their protest against the election of Aaron Shapiro as president. Shapiro, they wrote, "was a stranger both to the Yale community and to the values and principles which Yale University was founded to promote." The press release was designated for the wire services, national newspapers, and *The Yale Daily News.* It would reach them by telegrams dispatched for delivery early Monday at the same time Humber's similar messages with identical texts would reach national radio and television news offices. Humber and Mound, as Mound said to his collaborator, were hoping "to make a helluva stink." At the very least, as Humber had replied, they would embarrass Prox Young and Shapiro by forcing the story of the election to break before either was ready for it. In fact, Humber hoped their stratagem would force an annulment of the election. He still wanted fiercely to be president of Yale himself.

Unknowingly Aaron Shapiro assisted the plot by depositing his sons with his sister in New York City for the weekend while he moved in with Betty Barnard in Stamford for a few days. Consequently when Prox Young tried to reach him Saturday afternoon and Sunday, the only response he received was from Aaron's answering machine, inviting him to leave a message after the beep.

At seven o'clock Monday morning, while he was listening to the world news at breakfast, an hour before he planned to call Shapiro again, Prox Young heard National Public Radio report the details of the telegram just received about the protest against the election of Aaron Shapiro as President of Yale University. Aghast, he opened his copy of the *Times*, delivered to his door an hour earlier, and found the story on the front page, first column on the left. "Shit!" he exclaimed, his color rising. "Those SOBs!" It was, he realized at once, too late for a denial. The problem would be damage control. Reaching for the telephone, he dialed Arthur Stiles. He needed to consult the wisest man he knew.

The news about the election of Aaron Shapiro and the Humber-Mound protest spread through New Haven like a virulent flu. A special edition of *The Yale Daily News* ran a leader in large type reading "DOCTOR WHO?" The accompanying story argued that there must have been more desirable inside candidates. The *News* also attacked Dean Humber for treating a Yale issue as a national crisis. The Fellows, the *News* wrote, had failed to consult students who could not have been more indiscreet than Archibald Mound had been. The episode, so the editors argued, demonstrated the need for reforming the governance of the university to allow for more student power. As for Dr. Shapiro, the *News* withheld final judgment until he could be interviewed.

In the private conversations of disappointed aspirants to the presidency, judgments were not withheld. As Lilith Furman could have told them before the fact, men, when they feel rejected, turn for comfort to the women who love them. Tony Celotto, much upset when he heard the same broadcast that surprised Prox Young, threw on some clothes and drove over to see his mother who lived above her store. "Ma," he told her in high agitation, "I would never have thought of myself for the job if Mr. Young hadn't said I was his favorite. Then he and the others go and pick an outsider and dump me. So maybe someone doesn't like Italian-Americans? But then why a Jewish doctor? What do they take me for? I have feelings. Damned if I like having a strange doctor at 43 Hillhouse!"

Mrs. Celotto gave Tony a cup of black Italian espresso. "Here," she said. "Drink this. Your head got too big. You'll feel better in a few days."

"I don't know, Ma," Tony replied, "but I won't dump on you again."

Gene Barnard felt as if his insides had fallen out when he read the news in his morning *New Haven Register*. He spilled his daily glass of orange juice as he rushed from his kitchen and, without thinking, ran two doors to the house of Sylvia Wheatley who awoke when she heard him pounding up the stairs. "Sweetheart," he cried, "those bastards on the corporation have elected some unknown doctor to be president. How could they have done this to me? How could they have done this to Yale? To hell with them all." He fell onto her bed and into her arms. As she held him close, he moved his head down to her breasts, opened her nightie and mouthed her nearer nipple. She caressed him gently until, his sobbing spent, he began wordlessly to make love.

Both Jerry Walsh and Lilith Furman were shocked by the recklessness of Humber's action. "He's an egomaniac," Jerry said when he called her to compare notes.

"Maybe," Lilith replied. "Carter thinks Humber gets it off by picking fights, and he's probably also hooked on revenge."

"He's going to fall on his face," Jerry predicted. "We can be grateful at least that the Fellows chose a good man. We just could have done without the public controversy."

"I hope it won't persuade Shapiro to turn us down," Lilith said.

"Let's count on Prox and the King to take care of that," Jerry said. "I'll keep you posted if I hear anything. Do the same, will you? See you soon." Turning to Karen, who was sitting next to him at the kitchen table, he said, "I'm sure you heard all of that. I wish I were as confident about Shapiro as I sounded. Say, Gene Barnard must be in orbit!"

Karen, who had kept her word to Betty and said nothing to Jerry about Betty's involvement, replied blandly, "Yes, and Dr. Shapiro must have lots on his mind, too."

Indeed he did.

At a little after eight that morning, Proxmire Young reached Aaron Shapiro. "We all feel awful about what's happened," Prox said. "As you will know from your answering machine, I've been trying to reach you, but I did not expect the morning papers to beat me to it, or Archie Mound to kick up such a fuss."

"I've barely begun the account in the *Times*," Shapiro said. "I got home too late to call you last night, but I had surmised that you were going to tell me what the *Times* reported about your decision. The flap is regrettable, but it won't deter me if I decide to accept your offer."

"Thank goodness for that," Prox said. "Arthur Stiles, with whom I just talked, predicted you would react that way. I'm grateful. But I'm equally eager to have you accept. If you wish, I can now give you details about salary, fringe benefits and various perks, or if you prefer, I'll try to answer any questions you want to ask. Most of all, both my colleagues on the Corporation and I want you at Yale. And President Stiles is ready to talk freely with you at your convenience."

"I do want to see him," Shapiro said. "I'd also like to see more of the campus, including the medical school. And since the cat is out of the bag, I'd like to meet some representative faculty. Could we arrange all that for next Saturday?"

"Sure thing," Prox said. "President Stiles thought you would like to visit, and he suggested you spend Friday night with him as his guest, with a private dinner at your preferred hour, perhaps seven. Then he and I will set up a meeting at breakfast with the acting provost. President Stiles will be going to Princeton that morning, but you will have the full use of the president's residence. If you'd like, Dean Montefiore can meet you, I'm sure, to show you the medical school after breakfast, and I can arrange for Professor Gerald Walsh, whom you've met, of course, to take you around the campus and to introduce you to others at Yale you would like to meet. Perhaps you would like also to meet the others on Walsh's committee."

"That sounds just right," Shapiro replied, "I'd value some time with them, and Noah Montefiore is an old friend. Could you add to the list any of the local Yale people you were considering seriously for the appointment? I'd like to begin to make them easy with me. I'll need them, I'm sure, if I take the job, as I expect to, so don't worry. I simply want some time and some further introduction in order to be sure."

"Of course," Prox said. "How would it be if we ended the official part of the day with a small reception in the late afternoon for the faculty committee plus two of the men on our short list? I see no point in involving Robert Humber, the Dean of the Law School. I think you'll agree after reading the *Times* that his usefulness is over."

"I've read enough already to agree," Shapiro said. "May I ask who the other two are?"

"One is Anthony Celotto, the secretary of the university," Prox answered. "The other is Professor Eugene Barnard, a member of both the classics and the history departments."

"Interesting," Shapiro replied, thinking at once of Betty. "Let's proceed just as we've agreed. I'll call you if I have further thoughts, and I would appreciate it if you would fax me the proposed terms for salary and the like. Then I can study them before we meet. If the press calls, I intend to say no comment as often as necessary, though I see no point in denying I've received your offer. Will I have some private time with you Saturday?"

"Yes," Prox said. "How about after the reception? You're exactly right about the press, and I'll do the same."

"Good," Shapiro said.

"Some of the other Fellows may want to call you," Prox said, "and Arthur Stiles surely will. Is that okay?"

"Yes, of course," Shapiro said. "But please tell them that they are not to worry about the leak or the protest. I can take those things. And tell them, too, please not to turn on the charm to try to make me make up my mind. I won't until after next Saturday. Otherwise I'll gladly talk to them outside of business hours, preferably at home in the evening after eight and before ten. Except Wednesday when I must be in New York for a dinner at NYU."

"Thank you so much," Prox said. "Now I'll leave you alone." As Prox hung up, Aaron's thoughts returned to Betty. She had not told him that her husband was a candidate for the Yale presidency. But then they had not discussed him. She had said specifically that she did not want to. Now she had gone to visit her mother in Florida for a week. Aaron hesitated to call Betty there because she had told him she did not want him to. But on reflection he decided he had to in case she had read or heard about Archie Mound's calculated indiscretion.

Whenever she visited her mother, Betty Barnard felt as if she were in a space capsule. Her mother had a lifetime interest in a two-bedroom apartment, with meals and medical care provided and golf and swimming available, in a retirement home in Naples, Florida. For Betty, there was an unreality about Naples with its dozens of golf courses, its highrise condominiums and their narrow views of sandy beaches and blue-green water. There was a depressing unreality about the gerontological gentility of the retirement home, a depressing unreality about the morbidity and mortality of that environment. In her displaced state, Betty lost track of her normal interests, of her professional life, even of time itself. She did not read the newspaper because she had no interest in local news. She rarely listened to the radio or watched television. Indeed she avoided contact with normality in order to concentrate on satisfying her mother's incessant needs and on suffering silently the older woman's self-centered peccadilloes. She also privately counted the hours until she could leave.

Before departing Connecticut, Betty had described her bitter Florida mood to Aaron and urged him not to call or write. Her mother, she explained, thought that her daughter's marriage was ideal. It would upset her to learn the truth, particularly to learn that a divorce was pending and that another man, a stranger, had come into her daughter's life. It was best, Betty believed, to separate the reality of her life from the artificiality of her mother's existence and her own semiannual sojourns to that sad state.

So it came to Betty as a surprise when her mother, their card game interrupted by the telephone, said impatiently that a Doctor Shapiro was asking for her. "Who is he?" her mother inquired as Betty reached to pick up the receiver. "Later," Betty whispered, raising her voice as she spoke to Aaron. "Good morning, Doctor," she said crisply. "What may I do for you?"

"I take it this is not a good time to talk," Aaron answered, disappointment in his tone. "I know you told me not to call, but a matter of some importance has come up, as your morning newspaper perhaps reported, and I took the chance of violating your instructions."

"I haven't seen the newspaper," Betty said, "but perhaps you can tell me briefly what's on your mind."

"Well, to put it in a nutshell," Aaron replied, "Yale has asked me to be its next president."

Betty was stunned. Aaron, she had known, was on the list of men Yale was considering, but because she had assumed that the Yale Corporation would never select a Jew, she had discussed the matter with him only jokingly. Now she had to tell him how impossible it would be for her to see him as a lover in New Haven, how hostile she felt toward both the university and the city, how both evoked unhappy memories and associations, how both threatened her sense of privacy and security. But she could not say those things with her mother within earshot. Determined to keep her mother in the dark, Betty hoped Aaron would penetrate the code she decided to employ in answering him.

"That development comes as something of a surprise," she said. "I would advise you to delay a response until we can review the probable tax consequences of your decision. Surely the matter can wait until I see you as planned."

Now Aaron hesitated. Betty was telling him to wait, he realized, but her references to tax consequences left him rather puzzled about her true feelings. "As you recommend," he told her, "I'll await our meeting unless I'm pressed. I apologize for bothering you during your holiday. But surely considerations of security do not preclude my telling you as I hang up that I love you very much."

"That message is reciprocal," Betty said as their conversation ended. She took a deep breath, turned to her mother, and said she was sorry one of her clients had needed her advice at once. Her mother clucked her disapproval and complained about the delay the telephone had caused in the gin rummy game they were playing. As she silently discarded a jack of clubs, Betty began to think about how to explain her objections to Yale and New Haven to Aaron when he met her at LaGuardia Airport on the coming Sunday.

For his part, Aaron decided not to worry about Betty's cryptic response until he saw her. She had, after all, said that she loved him, and suffused as he was by his adoration of Betty, he expected love to conquer all.

Aaron Shapiro had a wonderful time during his day at Yale. On Friday evening when he came downstairs from his guest room at 43 Hillhouse, Arthur Stiles met him with a warm handshake and the offer of a drink. Aaron was no more than half way though his scotch on the rocks—the King had poured him at least three ounces of Glen Fiddich—before he decided that he liked his entertaining and welcoming host. Charlotte Stiles joined them only for dinner—a fresh green salad, trout almandine, green beans, a chocolate mousse, coffee and a memorable bottle of Sancerre, all prepared and served splendidly. Over brandy the two men then talked for two hours about Yale. It was not the King's charm but his incisive analyses that persuaded Aaron that the university was basically in very good shape. As the King openly admitted, the alumni needed fondling, the budget needed cutting, and many buildings would need refurbishing. "But the fundamentals," so the King put it, "are excellent—an outstanding faculty whose ablest members are still a decade or more from retirement, a superior student body, and a strong sense of common purpose."

At breakfast Saturday the acting provost and his senior associate presented figures and explained existing priorities that confirmed the King's observations. Noah Montefiore then drove Shapiro to the medical school where they talked for some time about current research by the faculty there and inspected some of the labs and parts of the Yale-New Haven Hospital. They then walked up to Mory's for luncheon with Jerry Walsh. Noah and Jerry tried to convince Aaron that the quaint institution that was Mory's, though a private club, served as a desirable alternative to a faculty club. Though unpersuaded, Aaron was amused by their parochialism and their avid defense of a menu no cardiologist would approve.

The early afternoon passed quickly because Jerry took Aaron to the art gallery where the extraordinary quality of the collections amazed him. He could not help but linger over the paintings, especially the superb examples of both Renaissance and modern masters. Little time remained for a quick inspection of the main library and a few of the treasures in the Beinecke Rare Book Library, a building that was a gem in itself.

Just after four o'clock, in an ebullient mood, Aaron Shapiro arrived with Jerry and Lilith Furman, who had joined them at Beinecke, for the small reception in the office of the secretary of the university. Noah Montefiore, pleading a developing cold, had begged off after luncheon, but otherwise the rest of the expected guests had preceded them. Aaron greeted those he had previously met by name, an impressive display of memory and preparation. Jerry then introduced Tony Celotto and Gene Barnard. Gene bowed slightly and walked away, his face a study in envy.

"I've been eager to talk to you," Aaron said to Tony. "I need to learn much more than I've yet been told about the duties of your office. President Stiles did say how admirably you handled them, and I can say without hesitation that I'm sure the next president will need your help."

"That's kind of you," Tony said, rather coolly in spite of his determination to show no emotion. "I'll be happy to see you at your convenience. My own plans are still uncertain. But now I must get my secretary to pass some drinks." He left in order to mobilize Isabel Doughton.

Alone for the moment, Aaron looked around the office. It was as generous as Noah had told him. He had come in through the big anteroom to the left off the hall of the ground floor of Woodbridge, and then through a small office where a heavy woman was seated at her serviceable desk. Just beyond the area in front of that desk, and through another door, Celotto's large desk stood angled away from the window behind it. The office had a north-south axis, with a fireplace on the south wall and a nearby door to what seemed to be a closet. Above a mahogany table against the east wall there was hanging in a broad, gilt frame, an oil portrait of a man Aaron could not identify. He proved on later inspection to be Reuben Holden, a former secretary of the university. All in all, Aaron thought, a most attractive office. He wondered if the president's was as handsome.

Seeing that Shapiro was alone, Roger Gordon, accompanied by Charlie Lee, came up to him and asked whether he would like a drink. The three then moved to the table where Isabel Doughton had placed two bottles of sherry and one of dry vermouth, some ice and glasses. Jerry Walsh, who was standing there, began pouring drinks, assisted by Gordon, with the others gathering around except for Gene Barnard who, arms akimbo and nose in the air, sat on the right edge of Tony's desk. Just then Miss Doughton said in a loud, surprised voice, "Hey, what do you think you're doing?"

In walked Bob Humber. "You must know," he said to Isabel, "that at last Banquo's ghost has arrived. Aren't you all pleased?" No one stirred. Undeterred, Humber asked, "Isn't anyone going to offer me a drink?" He started across the room to the drinks table.

"Given what you're full of," Roger Gordon said, "would you prefer castor oil or milk of magnesia?"

"I'm sure you'd rather give me poison," Humber replied. Then, turning to Aaron Shapiro, he continued, "Ah, you must be the good Hebrew doctor. I'm sure you must also have learned the local party line by now. Can you tell me how many liberals it takes to change a light bulb? No? The answer is that no one knows because liberals can't see the light."

"Get the hell out of here," Gordon said, "or I'll see you out."

"Now, now, Rogers, you revert to your caveman status too easily," Humber said, retreating. "I'm going to leave as soon as I tell Shapiro there that he'll need a new law dean if and when he arrives at 43 Hillhouse."

"Please don't leave," Aaron Shapiro said, "at least not before you've had a drink. I'd appreciate talking to you about your reasons for coming. I have lots to learn about Yale."

"Okay.," Humber said. "Until you're ready, I'll join Barnard in the exiles' corner." He moved to Celotto's desk and sat on its front left edge.

"Come on, guys," Lilith said. "Let's everyone relax. Gene and Bob, I'll get you some sherry. It's Harvey's Amontillado, and it will be good for you." She reached across to the table, poured two glasses, and turned back toward the men on the desk.

While Lilith was delivering the sherry, Jerry decided some further diversion was needed. "Gentlemen," he said, loudly enough to be heard over the murmuring in the room, "our guest has never seen the president's collar, and neither have I except from afar. Maybe Tony would display it for us."

"Would you like that?" Tony asked Aaron.

"Please. I know from Mr. Young that it exists, and I'd much enjoy seeing it."

While Tony moved to the vault that opened just outside his office in front of Isabel's desk, an expectant silence filled the room. Tony removed a wooden box, carried it to his desk behind which he stood, then opened the box, took out its contents, and placed them on his desk blotter. All eyes focused on the bejeweled, gold collar which lay glistening on a dark blue, velvet cloth. "Herewith," Tony said.

The room rustled with movement while everyone there tried to get a good look at the collar. As they all began to return, now murmuring their appreciation, to places and conversations they had left, Jerry walked to the fireplace, rapped on his glass for attention, and began a short impromptu toast. "Dr. Shapiro is here to look us over, and I'm sure we all hope we pass his muster. I would like to thank him for coming, and to ask you to drink to his permanent return and to our university."

"To Yale," Tony said, raising his glass. Several voices said, "hear, hear."

It was just then, with everyone looking at Jerry and lifting a glass, that the impulse overcame the thief. Without thinking about what he was doing, he reached his hand out to the collar, picked it up gently, and quickly dropped it into the poacher's pocket inside his Harris tweed jacket.

The collar just fit the space designed for a couple of rabbits some imaginary poacher had shot on the private estate of an equally imaginary Scot laird. The collar weighed so much that the thief put his left hand into his trouser pocket in order to press the collar against his hip so as to keep the jacket from drooping with the burden it now held. Glancing about surreptitiously, the thief breathed a sigh of mixed triumph and relief. No one, he was sure, had observed him, but now the collar would be worn by no one else.

After the toast the reception began to near its end. Barnard and Humber left first. Then Lilith said goodbye to Aaron Shapiro and started home to her waiting husband. Charlie Lee and Roger Gordon followed her. Aaron told Jerry that Proxmire Young was awaiting him at 43 Hillhouse, and after thanking Tony for his hospitality, he left.

"Isabel and I will clean up," Tony told Jerry. "Go on along if you like."

"Where is she?" Jerry asked.

"She went back to her own office a little while ago," Tony replied. "She'll return when I call her."

"Then thanks, I will go," Jerry said. "It's been a long day. I'm sure it hasn't been easy for you either."

"I'll get used to it," Tony said, reaching out to open the box for the collar. "Oh my God, Jerry," he bellowed as he examined the box and frantically case his eyes over the surface of his desk, "the collar's gone."

"Let's look on the floor," Jerry suggested calmly. They did, and they examined the vault, all the furniture, and even looked under all the cushions. Tony again called out to Isabel, but she had obviously departed, probably to go home. "I'll be damned," Jerry finally said. "It is gone. Tony, let's keep mum about this until we've consulted the King." He picked up Tony's phone.

Two hours later at 43 Hillhouse, the King's study was crowded. He sat at his desk with Jerry Walsh and Tony Celotto on flanking chairs. Across from the president were the general counsel of the university, Christopher Marshall, and the chief of the Yale police, Henry Fawcett. Marshall, a recent graduate of the college and law school where he had been an editor of the law journal, had come to Yale from the Central Intelligence Agency only a few months earlier. He had been in that agency's contract division where his legal responsibilities had nothing to do with cloak and dagger work. Fawcett, the first black man to hold the job, had become Yale's chief four years previously. The group, summoned by Arthur Stiles after Jerry had called him, had been conferring for an hour and a half.

"You agree, then," the King said, "that only someone who was at the reception could have stolen the collar, and only Yale faculty were there except for Tony, who is one of us, and Aaron Shapiro, who may become one of us. In any case, there is no reason to even suspect Shapiro. I do not want a scandal. I do not want even by indirection to have anyone who was there under public suspicion as a thief. So I do not want anyone from the outside involved in this unfortunate development."

"Tony said Isabel Doughton was also there," Fawcett interrupted.

"She was in and out of my office," Tony said. "I can't recall where she was at any one time, except she'd gone when we discovered the collar missing."

"She has been at Yale so long that I regard her as if she were faculty. She's an Old Blue as far as I'm concerned," the King said.

"But she is also a suspect like everyone else, except, as you say, Dr. Shapiro," Fawcett said. "We really do not yet know when the theft occurred."

"But you're going to find out, Henry," the King said. "I want you in charge of an internal investigation. You are not to inform the city police. Under no conditions do I intend the university to press charges against anyone who was there. So we are going to handle this matter ourselves, and we are going to be wholly discreet. I want your word about that, all of you. Henry, I want you to begin at once. Any comments? Christopher, any objections?"

Marshall had none. The others remained silent except for Fawcett. "Mr. President," he said, "I must warn you that the city police will be furious if we keep them out of this. But I'll play it your way. And I'll interview Professor Walsh and Mr. Celotto this evening, if they are willing, but it's Saturday and the others may be hard to locate without the kind of fuss you want me to avoid. I'll get to them first thing tomorrow."

"I want you to proceed as you think best but without the city people," the King replied.

"Tony and I have told you just about all we know," Jerry said, "but I'm ready to talk to you privately as long as you like. I'd like a chance to eat first."

"Me too," Tony said.

"You work it out with Henry," Arthur Stiles said. "Thank you all for coming. Now this meeting is over."

Aaron Shapiro and Prox Young had met only for a moment at 43 Hillhouse before they walked back to Mory's where Prox had booked a private room for dinner. During the meal he reviewed the financial terms of Yale's offer. Aaron considered them eminently fair, even generous, as he said, promising also to let Prox know his decision by Tuesday at the latest. That would give him time to talk to Betty. The two men parted a little after eight that evening, both wholly unaware of the theft of the necklace and the ensuing meeting. The King intended for the time being to keep it that way. As he had said at the meeting, there was no reason to put Prox Young in orbit.

So Aaron had only positive thoughts about his day at Yale when on Sunday morning he drove to LaGuardia Airport to meet Betty Barnard's plane, due at noon from Naples. But he knew he had to find out why Betty had urged him to delay any commitment. They embraced when Betty entered the terminal and then walked quickly to retrieve her luggage and pick up Aaron's car.

While Aaron steered through the heavy traffic on Long Island on their way back to Betty's place in Stamford, they both self-consciously avoided the question most on their minds. Instead they chatted about Betty's mother, whose advancing years and deteriorating temperament suggested the onset of senility. Once on the New York Throughway, driving northeast toward Connecticut on a highway almost empty, Aaron at last, though obliquely, raised the vital subject.

"Dearest," he said, "I was in New Haven all day yesterday, looking around Yale. I even met your uncivil husband who has no idea I know you. But he must have wanted to be president of Yale very much. He just about cut me cold. He knew, you see, that I had been asked to be the next president of that university."

"Oh, Aaron, love, please no!" Betty cried, her pent-up tension bursting forth. "I've been upset ever since you telephoned me. You never even consulted me. We should have talked about it long ago. I blame myself for not doing so. But no! Please no."

"But why not?" Aaron replied, stunned by her response. "Hey, I haven't accepted the job. I'm consulting you right now. I thought you'd be proud of me. I thought we'd get married after your divorce is final, and then you could go on with your law firm but also take over at Yale affairs when it suited your convenience as first lady. Why not?"

"Aaron, you don't face reality," Betty said. "I do love you, but I've never agreed to marry you. I've even told you that I'm not ready for another marriage, and I don't know when or whether I will be. And I hope I never have to live in New Haven again, or have to have anything to do with Yale. I've had all I can take of that scene. Gene ruined it for me. Even if he hadn't, I couldn't be a Charlotte Stiles. I've other things to do, things more important to me. No, Aaron, it's out of the question. Go ahead if you must, but not with me. I'd hate not to see you any more, but if you take that job, you leave me with no choice."

Aaron reflected silently for what seemed to Betty a long time, in fact less than two minutes. "Betty," he then asked, "would you move in with me if I stayed in Dobbs Ferry? I could explain it to the boys. They're old enough now. Then some day if things worked out to your taste, we could talk about getting married. You're vastly more important to me than the Yale presidency is."

"Aaron, darling, could we just go on as we are for now?" Betty answered. "After the divorce is over with we can talk about it some more. I want to be part of your life, but don't push me too hard. I'm pretty fragile."

"I'll settle for that without further argument," Aaron said.

"And give up Yale?" Betty asked.

"And gladly give up that kingdom for the woman I love," Aaron said, leaning over and kissing her nose.

"Hey, you, watch where you're going," Betty said, her voice filled with the relief she felt and the love for Aaron she had been afraid he might spurn when she balked at sharing his new opportunity.

"I'm going to take you home," Aaron replied, at peace at once with his decision, "and then just you try to get rid of me. I'll call Proxmire Young first thing tomorrow morning. He'll have a fit. But first you and I will sleep on it."

"Oh, yes," Betty said, sliding closer.

9.
DEVELOPMENTS

Sunday evening the thief rejoiced. Chief Fawcett had not in the least challenged his story during the grilling that afternoon. It had been an impulsive, even a stupid, act, but the thief had no regrets. In any event, it was too late to try safely to return the collar. Now, his spirits rising, he believed he was going to get away with it. He would soon make his way to a pawnshop he knew in East Haven, and there he could be completely anonymous while he sold the collar for its worth in gold and jewels. He did not need the money but he could not credibly refuse it. For the time being, he hid the collar in the basket of ironing that awaited the attention of the Thursday maid.

Sunday evening the witness also rejoiced. The chief had come and gone, and apparently suspected nothing. Early Monday morning the witness, using a simple but private code, typed a description of the theft on the computer. The information was secure there because only the witness knew the code name necessary to access the relevant file. The information would reside invulnerably where it was until the witness found it convenient to retrieve it. Then payday would lie ahead.

10.
BLUE MONDAY

For several of the favorite sons of mother Yale, Sunday's events forecast a blue Monday. For Prox Young Monday began with the telephone call from Aaron Shapiro declining the presidency. Shapiro was utterly candid. He was proud of having received the offer, he said, and he hated rejecting it. He was also distressed that he had wasted Yale's time. But he had to bow to the wishes of his beloved. He should have consulted her sooner, but it had not occurred to him to do so. Prox could tell from the tone of Shapiro's voice that argument would be futile. He immediately told the King what had happened. On his advice, Prox then called all the Fellows he could reach and set up an emergency meeting of the Corporation for Wednesday in New York. Most of them could attend and all of them pledged secrecy. There would be no announcement until they had decided on their next course.

For Lilith Furman, Monday began with a telephone call from Chief Fawcett arranging an appointment that morning about an undefined emergency. She and her husband, Carter Jefferson, had been in Boston Sunday to see friends there. Fawcett had therefore interviewed all the others who had attended Saturday's reception for Aaron Shapiro and left Lilith for last. The accounts he had received from Jerry Walsh and Tony Celotto on Saturday coincided, as also had those from the other men whom he had seen on Sunday. He expected more of the same from Lilith, but of course he had to be sure. Someone, after all, had stolen the collar, and no one had admitted to it. The chief had checked with Arthur Stiles about insurance. Yale, he discovered, had no insurance on the collar, so no insurance investigator would complicate Fawcett's own inquiry.

But the hope to avoid publicity had proved futile by Monday morning. Right after the chief had left him Sunday, Robert Humber called Archie Mound to inform him. As Humber had expected, Mound, hoping to embarrass the university, at once telephoned the *Chicago Tribune* to report the theft and criticize what he called Yale's "inadequate security system." The wire services carried the news that night. Since Yale did not officially acknowledge the matter, the New Haven police left it alone. The mayor, who had little use for Yale, told the city chief of police that it would be good for the university to stew in its own broth. Arthur Stiles was privately grateful for that unintended favor.

Detective Lieutenant Deno Stavros, infuriated by the news about Yale's attempted secrecy, knew nothing about the mayor's decision. On his own, he called Chief Fawcett to give him hell. "You goddam Yalies," Stavros yelled into his telephone, "you got the bright idea you have your own law. Listen up, Chief, you got a thief in your snotty university. He already stole the jewelry. That's grand larceny. You try to handle it yourself, pretty soon you gonna be trying to conceal rape and murder. You should'a called me in. You're gonna be sorry. For now you can damn well hang out to dry, you're so wet behind the ears."

Stavros banged down the phone before Fawcett could reply. Frustrated, Fawcett could feel his own adrenalin pumping. He was angry, but he suspected that Stavros was right. Feeling chagrined, he calmed down while walking over to see Lilith Furman. She was reading about the theft in the morning papers when Fawcett arrived at her office. "Hi, Henry," she said, "now I know what's eating you. Honest, I didn't do it."

"It's no joke, Lil," Fawcett replied. "Look, we're pals, but I have to treat you as a witness, and I'm going to record what you say, as I have with all the others. So begin when you're ready."

"I've been thinking about the collar since I began reading the paper," Lilith said. "To the best of my memory, everyone on the faculty advisory committee—you know about that, I'm sure—was there except for Dean Montefiore when Dean Humber arrived. So were Tony Celotto, Professor Barnard and Dr. Shapiro. We were all sort of standing around, overhearing Tony and Gene being rude to Shapiro. Humber came in and began to pick fights. He moved back to Tony's desk when Roger Gordon told him off. He sat on one corner of the desk, with Gene Barnard sitting on the other. Isabel Doughton had gone to bring in the drinks and then, I think, left again. Jerry Walsh had suggested that Dr. Shapiro and the rest of us might like to see the collar, and Tony had fetched the box that holds it from the vault. Tony stood right behind his desk, guarding the collar and the box, it seemed. We'd all had a look and then dropped back to let others see. Before Humber and Gordon could resume their spat, Jerry went over to the fireplace and tried to ease things by offering a toast to Dr. Shapiro. At that point everyone looked at Jerry, as I remember, and we had the toast. I'm going to guess that it was then that the collar was stolen. But most of us were too far away to reach it. Only Tony, Gene, and Humber, all of them at the desk, were near enough. I was at the other end of the room in front of Jerry. Professors Lee and Gordon were with Dr. Shapiro just behind me. Jerry was at the hearth. So as I say, no one except those at the desk was near the collar."

Lilith stopped for a few seconds to catch her breath. "Of course," she went on, "someone may have stolen it on his way out of the office. I think I was among the first to leave. I have no memory of looking at the box or the collar on my way out."

"What you say conforms with what everyone else has told me," the chief said. "Do you remember whether the box was open or closed after you all had examined the collar?"

Lilith though a bit and replied, "I have absolutely no idea."

"Neither does Tony," the chief said. "He recalls his shock when he saw that the collar was gone, but neither he nor Jerry remember whether Tony had to open the box to find out. I suspect not, but it's an interesting detail in a story I have to reconstruct. This much is clear: someone is lying. Otherwise, frankly, I'm at sea, and I need your help and Jerry's."

"So we're cleared?" Lilith asked.

"Everyone I've talked to places you out of the picture during the toast, and I can't believe you took the collar on your way home. You don't take chances like that, and you'd have been too eager to get to Carter. Anyhow, character counts with me, and I've never suspected you."

"Thanks, Henry," Lilith said. "Has Jerry enough character?"

"Of course," Fawcett said, "but I checked him out. He was near the door going out of the office while the rest of you were leaving. He'd moved there to say goodbye to Dr. Shapiro. Then later, while Tony went to the men's room, Jerry called the King. They walked over to 43 Hillhouse together. I was with them while the King instructed us. Then I patted down Tony and Jerry before I questioned them. They were clean. Jerry couldn't have left the collar anywhere, but Tony could have hidden it in the men's room, though my men didn't find it when they looked there and everywhere else in Woodbridge Hall. Tony was so close to his desk that I have to keep him on my list of suspects even though he is my boss. But as far as I'm concerned, Jerry is as innocent as you are."

"You said you needed our help," Lilith said. "In what way, may I ask; though of course I'll do anything I can."

"There's no point in grilling the faculty types again," Fawcett said. "They're not afraid of me. Whoever is lying is not about to stop. But they'll get lazy about what they say in conversations with each other and with their friends. So I want you and Jerry to keep your ears open, and to let me know everything you hear, no matter how trivial it seems. I'm willing to bet the theft wasn't planned. Someone just grabbed at a lucky chance, maybe for profit, maybe just to be mean. But someone is going to get careless, I predict, and then we'll move in. For now we have to be patient."

"One question," Lilith said. "You can count on our cooperation, but what about with Tony's secretary. Is she clear?"

"I've confirmed to my satisfaction that she'd gone to her own office before the collar was taken," Fawcett replied, "and then gone home before you all left. So she's as clean."

He thanked Lilith, and departed. But his best hopes did not materialize. No one got careless during the following days.

As he was about to leave his office late Wednesday afternoon, Jerry Walsh received a telephone call from Proxmire Young. "The Fellows have been meeting since this morning at the Century," Prox said, "and we've reached some decisions that you need to know about. I've just asked the King about them and he agrees. First, prepare yourself for a shock. Aaron Shapiro turned us down on Monday."

"I can't believe it," Jerry interrupted. "He seemed one of us last Saturday. What went wrong? Did he want more money or something like that?"

"Nothing like that," Prox replied, "and please be sure that your colleagues realize that money was in no way an issue. He said the woman he loved was opposed to his taking the job, and he had to honor her wishes."

"Who's the femme fatale?" Jerry asked, "and why in the world didn't he tell us sooner?"

"He hasn't told me her name. As I understand it, he hadn't asked her, so he didn't know," Prox said. "I gather the relationship between them is relatively new."

"I suppose then that we're up the creek. Are you going to ask one of the others on the short list?"

"That's what the Fellows have been discussing all day," Prox answered, "and that's why I'm calling you. The answer is no, we're not, so we have to proceed quickly to decide on a new candidate before Humber and Mound can raise much more hell. Most of us were at the meeting—only three of the fifteen couldn't make it, Mound of course, and Murphy and I forgot the third—and we were unanimous that I was to announce Shapiro's decision right away. I just have. I'll read you the press release in a minute. We also agreed that we did not really want the same short list. I think there would have been a ground swell for Sis Overman, but she insisted she would not consider the job. She'd been through that, she said, and wasn't going through it again.

You know, Jerry, I've come to admire that woman."

"So have I," Jerry said. "Lilith has from the beginning."

"To continue," Prox said, "the search committee members were all of the view that we'd given a lot of thought to Humber and he would not do. Everyone agreed. As for Tony, the Fellows were not enthusiastic. So we decided to keep Gene Barnard on a new list but to add some others before making a decision. The same old search committee is to get back to work. The others thought we'd proved our worth by finding Shapiro. And the committee members know how crucial a part your group played in that discovery, so the Fellows want your committee to reconvene and advise us again. Our aim is to have a working list by Christmas at the latest, and to appoint a president early next year. So we're sort of going back to the beginning, but now in something of a rush. The King is also going to feed us some names, and I hope your people will soon."

"I'll be glad to help," Jerry said, "but we are all pretty busy. The end of the term is coming. That means exams and papers and grades before the Christmas holidays. And Lilith and I are supposed also to be helping Chief Fawcett about the collar, though there's nothing much we can do about that except to be alert. But sure, we'll all do as much as we can to assist you."

"That damn collar!" Prox said. "I'll never understand how it could have been stolen. The theft hurt Tony's stock with the Fellows. He was in charge of it, after all."

"Shall I call my colleagues and tell them about Shapiro tonight?"

"Might as well do it ASAP," Prox said. "I'd rather your committee didn't read about it before learning about it. And I hope you'll be meeting again very soon."

"Done," Jerry said. "I'm sorry Shapiro declined, but Yale will survive."

"Agreed," Prox said. "Thanks, Jerry, and good night."

Jerry rang off. Karen would be astonished, he thought to himself, to find out what Shapiro had done and why.

"Hi, honey, I'm home. Better late than never," Jerry Walsh called out to Karen as he entered their house. "Where are you? I need a stiff drink."

"I'm in the kitchen," Karen called back. "Come give me a kiss."

Jerry complied enthusiastically. "Hey," Karen said, breaking his embrace, "do you want dinner or do you want to eat later?"

"I'd rather eat later," Jerry said. "But I've got some big news that will knock your eyes out. It means I have to live for a while on the phone as soon as we have a drink and eat. You won't believe it, but Shapiro told the corporation no. Prox just issued an announcement. It will be all over the papers tomorrow morning. I have to call the rest of the committee tonight so that they won't be surprised." He poured two vodkas on the rocks while talking.

"Add two drops of vermouth to mine," Karen said, "and explain, if you can, what went wrong. What's the corporation going to do now?"

"They are going to resume the search, try to identify some new possibilities, and reconvene our advisory committee. As if we had nothing else to do! But what's the alternative? And there's more."

"You expected Shapiro to accept," Karen said. "Was he put off by the collar business?"

"No," Jerry answered, "it's something very different. Officially he declined for 'family reasons.' Actually he told Prox that he was following the wishes of the woman he loves."

Karen gasped and her face turned white, as if all the blood had left her head. During the next few seconds of silence, Jerry expected her to faint. She did not, but she sat down at the kitchen table, put her head on her arms, and finally, in a whispering voice, said, "Oh, no! Oh, what has Betty done?"

Jerry stared at her, and she blushed. She had not meant to let him know that Betty was the woman.

"Betty? Betty Barnard? I'll be damned! That's the ultimate irony," Jerry said, gulping down his drink and pouring himself some more vodka. "I'm sure she didn't mean to, but she's revived Gene's candidacy by knocking out Shapiro. Don't repeat this, but Gene will be on the new short list. Want some more vodka?"

"No thanks. I've had enough, and so now have you," Karen said. "Come on, the casserole is ready. We can eat. Please set the table and I'll serve it. We'll stay right here and eat quickly. You can use the blue dinner plates. It's scallops, shrimp and wild rice, one of your favorites."

They sat for a time in silence while they thought about Betty and Gene. Then Jerry realized that Karen had known about Betty and Shapiro for some time. "Listen, dear," he said, "I don't want to pry, but weren't you keeping something from me? It must have had to do with Betty and Shapiro. Any more secrets? I'd hate to see us recommend another candidate whose love life got in his way.

"Now you know my last secrets," Karen replied. "Betty and Dr. Shapiro, and Gene and Sylvia. But please keep them to yourself. I feel awful for telling you."

"They'll be safe with me," Jerry said. Then, reaching for the phone, he began to call the members of his committee. Karen could overhear him saying much the same thing to each man he informed, always protecting Betty's anonymity. He called Lilith last. She listened without comment until he finished. "You don't know who the woman is," she said, "or we could try working on her."

"Too late, I'm sure," Jerry replied. "We're back to the hunt."

"I've been thinking while you were talking," Lilith said. "We know some good men we haven't really looked at hard. Dick Mason for one. He has the solidity Shapiro has but we just let him plead off. I'm going to suggest him to the committee Sunday. Why don't you see whether he's at all flexible? And why not see the King about able outsiders?"

"I'm going to leave the King to Prox," Jerry replied. "And I'd rather see what response you get from our committee about Dick before I lean on him. I don't mind telling you that I still don't rule Gene out, especially if the corporation is really in an almighty hurry. You and I also have the damn collar to think about. Should we plan luncheon later this week?"

"I'm terribly busy this week," Lilith said. "I'll call you if anything occurs to me about the collar. Right now I agree with Henry Fawcett that one of the three who were at the desk during your toast is the likely culprit, but I don't know where to begin to find out which. And I don't want Tony or Gene to be guilty. I'd like to pin it on Humber, but that's not fair."

"I'm with you," Jerry said. "Maybe we had better concentrate now on a good night's sleep. Thanks for your time."

Turning to Karen who was yawning at the kitchen table, he said, "I'd give up Yale for you if it ever came to that." Karen smiled and kissed him.

Proxmire Young's announcement naturally fueled new speculation about developments at Yale. Both the *Yale Daily News* and the *New Haven Register* interpreted Dr. Shapiro's rejection of the presidency as a major blow to the university's prestige. "For God, for Country and for Yale," Harry Grayson wrote, made no allowances for exemptions "for family reasons." If Shapiro felt otherwise, he went on, he should never have been chosen. Students, had they been consulted, would not have selected other than a real Yale man. The *Register* and Channel 8 TV News considered Shapiro's decision an unwarranted rejection of New Haven. The choice of a local resident, they held, would have prevented the slight to the city's pride. The *New York Times* interpreted the decision to invite Shapiro as an indication of the increased prominence of medicine in higher education and its complex financing. An op ed piece later in the week argued that the administration of higher education had become such a burden that it was bound to interfere with the family life of the president of any major university. The sacrifice, it implied, was both necessary and unavoidable.

For Robert Humber, Shapiro's decision revived the opportunity he had been seeking. He and Archie Mound began at once to circulate to all Yale alumni a petition urging the Corporation to elect Humber president. They were gratified that by Saturday they had assurances of a first hundred and fifty-two signatures. By the end of the following week they expected at least ten times that number. Charley Dray, when Humber told him about their early support, warned Prox Young that the search committee could not afford to dally.

Young had already begun to move as fast as he could. On Thursday morning he had called Arthur Stiles to ask whether he knew of any Yale alumnus who was doing an outstanding job as president of a good, small liberal arts college. The King called back an hour later to recommend David Benedict, president of Bassett College near Duluth, Minnesota. Benedict had a doctorate in English from Yale where he had served as an assistant professor and an assistant dean of the Graduate School of Arts and Sciences. In his five years at Bassett, he had succeeded in ridding the college of its fraternities and in instituting coeducation. The college had won some new acclaim as "the Williams of the north." So informed, Prox immediately invited Benedict to talk about the Yale presidency that Saturday with Sis Overman and Charley Dray in Washington. Benedict agreed with the understanding that the proposed meeting implied no commitment on either side.

In New Haven Humber's recourse to a petition encouraged Tony Celotto to see himself as again a viable candidate. Tony knew the Fellows well enough to be sure that any petition would serve only to irritate them. But the petition, he judged, would also hurry their deliberations, and he considered himself an obvious prospect for reconsideration. Taking an indiscreet chance, he phoned Lilith Furman, whom he trusted as a friend, to ask her, as a member of the faculty advisory committee, whether there was any basis for his hopes. Lilith knew there was not, but out of consideration for Tony's feelings, she hedged her answer. "I can't be sure," she said, "because our committee has yet to receive any precise directions from the Fellows' committee." That statement, as she realized, was both accurate and disingenuous. But Tony in his optimism accepted it as encouraging.

The announcement of Shapiro's decision had a powerful impact on Gene Barnard. As soon as he heard the morning radio news on Thursday, he called Sylvia Wheatley. "Listen, darling," Gene said, "Shapiro has turned Yale down! That means I have a chance, a good one. So we have to be careful again. I don't want anyone to have even a suspicion that you and I are close until the Fellows have decided on whom to choose. If they select me, as they should, and if all is going along well with the divorce, we can go public after I accept. We can announce our engagement. But until then, and it shouldn't be long, we had better not see each other, not even out of town. I'll hate it, but I'm sure I have to be prudent to a fault."

"I'll hate it, too," Sylvia replied. "Still, I want with all my heart for you to be president, and I believe we must not let anything get in the way. But if there's no decision by Christmas, couldn't we find some way to be together for the holiday? It would mean so much to both of us."

"Let's leave that question until the winter solstice," Gene suggested. "My guess is that we'll know by then. I love you, and I'll be thinking of you all the time we're apart. There's no reason we can't chat on the telephone, so I'll call you again later. I want now to try to pump Jerry Walsh."

Without waiting, Gene next called Jerry. "Look, old friend," Gene said, "I really dislike imposing on our relationship because it means a lot to me and I don't want to offend you. But I just heard about Dr. Shapiro. I have to admit to you that I'm excited about the possibility of having the Corporation turn to me. What I most want to know, so much so that I'm frantic, is whether there's a chance they might. So in complete confidence I'm begging you to tell me. You may be sure that I'll never repeat what you say."

Jerry said nothing while thinking about Gene's request. He did not want to violate the confidentiality of his committee's information. He also did not want to raise Gene's hopes too much. He wished Gene had not asked. He had thought Gene knew better. But he also understood the tensions that must have motivated the call, and he disliked letting a good friend down.

Jerry was still ruminating when Gene spoke up. "Hey, Jerry, you still there?"

"I'm thinking," Jerry said. "You know I should not tell you a thing. But I have a very good sense of the pressure you've put on yourself. Under no condition should you let your expectations get out of hand, but I will tell you that your name is on the short list. Now you must understand that guarantees nothing. Other names will be on that list, too. So go about your daily business without letting yourself think about what I've told you, and don't repeat it to anyone at all. And Gene, never ask me any further question about this matter, or we cannot remain friends. Now you shut up and I'll hang up."

Gene smiled in satisfaction. He now knew all he needed to know for the time being. He was going, he felt sure, to be the next president of Yale.

At breakfast Thursday the witness welcomed the news of Shapiro's decision as a magnificent opportunity. The thief would surely be excited and ripe for the plucking. The time had obviously come to take the next step. After trying several drafts, the witness settled on the one that seemed most threatening:

> *Your theft was observed. It would shatter your hopes if the wrong people learned about it. You can preserve silence with a first benediction of $5,000 in small unmarked bills mailed in a plain package to the post office box for Snoopy listed in Personals next Monday in the Register.*

The witness had rented the post box for just the use that had now become timely. The witness had also thought about telephoning the classified ad to the paper, but that would have entailed releasing the calling number and mailing a check in payment. So the witness had put on as a disguise some old painting clothes and a scarf that partially covered the face. The clerk would remember a slovenly blue-collar worker if the clerk remembered anything at all. Then the witness had driven to the *Register* and placed the notice in the classified section for Monday, Tuesday and Wednesday. The charge for classified ads covered three days, and the witness saw no danger in repetition. No one but the thief would understand the text of the ad:

Snoopy seeks solace. SWM or DWM only. PO Box 9026, New Haven, 06533.

The thief should have a package in the mail by next Wednesday, the witness estimated, with delivery a day later.

With a manifest lack of enthusiasm, the faculty advisory committee met according to plan Sunday afternoon in Jerry's office. Their deliberations started at once. "So, Noah," Charlie Lee asked, "how do you explain your friend's decision?"

"I'm as mystified as all of you," Noah Montefiore said. "I had no idea there was a woman in his life."

"Let's let bygones be bygones," Jerry said. "As I told all of you by phone, we're more or less back to square one. But not quite. Prox thinks Humber and Mound are dangerous, so he wants to develop a new short list and pick someone as fast as possible, and he has Gene Barnard as one man on the list. He called this morning to tell me he's also interested in a David Benedict, the president of Bassett College in Minnesota, whom the King recommended. Senator Overman and Charley Dray have interviewed him and think he's worth serious attention. Benedict has a Yale Ph.D. in English. He was around here for a while as an assistant professor and assistant dean. Some of you may have known him. I didn't. That's about as far as we've gone."

"Yeah, I knew him," Roger Gordon said. "He had our department as one of his responsibilities in graduate admissions. Always seemed to me pretty tight with fellowship money, but that wasn't his fault, I guess. There just wasn't much money. Decent enough guy, but sort of bland. Always cheerful but tough when he wanted to be. Seemed to me that he didn't know much about psychology except for the popular Freudian kind of stuff. I doubt he knew or cared why we used rats."

"That's a fair assessment, I think," Noah said. "Good field, no hit, again. A minor league Gene Barnard. I used to see Benedict on the liaison committee that Dick Mason appointed between the medical school and the graduate school. He was the keeper of our records. Didn't say much, but now and then I talked with him when we broke for a few minutes for coffee. I don't know anything about Bassett College, but he seems to me to be in his proper league there."

"Agreed," Gordon said. "The old problem remains the same. What about the next president and the sciences? We're right back where we were in September."

"I think so, too," Charlie Lee said. "So that makes three of us not satisfied with Barnard or Benedict."

"I don't think you've given them a decent chance," Jerry said. "No one of us has ever adequately examined either man. It's simply too soon to dismiss them."

"Okay, Noah and Charlie and I will talk to them," Roger Gordon said, "but I doubt it will make any difference. If Proxmire Young is in such a sweat, we need more names, including some scientists."

"I think I have a useful idea," Lilith said. "Dick Mason has the gravitas we liked in Dr. Shapiro. We know Dick, we know his record as provost, we know he's been promoting the sciences and medicine, we know he uses some pretty sophisticated math in his economics, we know he's a top administrator, and we know he's a Yale alumnus, same class as Gene Barnard, I think, What's more we know his wife, Martha, and she'd be superb in 43 Hillhouse. We've just taken his word for it that he's not interested. He needs to be pushed. If he knew he was a leading candidate, he might discover he was interested. And then he might prove to be less private and shy than Jerry says he is. We can't take anyone's word for it. We have to ask outright."

"Good idea," Charlie said, "Mason has the smarts. I worked over some physics budgets with him, and he knows his stuff."

"Look," Jerry said, "Dick is just as good a friend of mine as Gene is. I have the highest opinion of him, too. But I can't believe he wants the job."

"Why not find out directly?" Roger asked. "Lilith is right. Let Dick speak for himself."

"It's certainly worth a try," Noah said. "The worst he can say is no.

But should one of us talk to him for our committee, or should we throw some real weight around by lining up Proxmire Young before we see Dick?"

"The real test would have to involve the corporation," Lilith said. The others nodded, and Jerry replied, "Okay. Then we're agreed. How about I speak to Young tomorrow and let him do it, or let him have someone do it for him, if he's with us? I suspect he won't be able to move without consulting his search committee, but we can get him started in that direction."

"Why not tell him outright that Mason is the preferred choice of this faculty committee right now?" Roger asked.

"I'm not sure I agree with that," Jerry replied. "I still want more of a look-see for Gene."

"But I much prefer Mason," Charlie said, "and so do the rest of us."

"I'm with Charlie," Noah said.

"So am I," Roger said.

"I'm afraid I agree, Jerry," Lilith said.

"You win," Jerry conceded. "I'll put it to Prox as Roger suggested. But keep quiet about this. I'm reasonably sure Prox will wait to talk to his committee, and even if they agree in the end, it will take some time before anything definite happens."

"Good meeting," Roger said. "Now let's go home." No one objected to that motion.

After several efforts Jerry reached Proxmire Young about noon on Monday. "I get the message," Prox said when Jerry had finished reporting the conclusions of the faculty committee. "Of course I'll have to consult the rest of the search committee. I can say now that it's an idea worth pursuing. Mason has an excellent track record. But I want to think about whether his policies would be too much like the King's, and about whether he can reach the alumni. He's had some experience raising money for his class, so I'll look into that. I'll have some decision for you within a week. If we're going to pressure Mason, then I'll do it or get the King to do it. Thanks for your good work."

11.
SUSPENSE

Just about noon on Monday the thief found the witness's threat in his Yale mailbox. He read it through quickly, then over and over, his pulse racing faster as he read. "Get a grip on yourself," his inner voice warned. "You've got to think who could have seen it, who sent this goddamn note? How could anyone have seen what happened? Everyone was looking at Walsh. How serious is this demand? It's serious. No doubt about that. Get a grip on yourself. You need a drink." He walked in a black cloud to Mory's, asked for an empty table, sat down and ordered a double vodka on the rocks.

All afternoon and evening, the thief thought about the identity of the witness. One after another, his memory eliminated the men and the one woman who had been in Celotto's office. In his mind's eye, he could see Jerry Walsh at the table at the far end, Lilith Furman moving toward Walsh and past Shapiro and the brace of Gordon and Lee, then Walsh starting to the hearth, eyes turning toward him. Walsh was looking at Shapiro, the others at Walsh as he spoke. No one in the room, as the thief reconstructed the scene, could have seen him, for he moved so fast. So he must have been seen from the adjoining office. Just like that fat woman! She had gone in there and was probably standing at the door, spying. She was known for minding everyone else's business, for reading other people's mail, for poking her nose into university affairs. "Snoopy" indeed! How to put her off? He asked that question again and again through the evening and into his restless sleep.

It proved to be surprisingly easy, though worry had consumed much of the previous night. At eleven that morning it was simple to walk from the city parking lot on Broadway east to York Street and south down to Cedar Street, left there, along Cedar to the Sterling Hall of Medicine, then into the medical school and laboratories. Memory served well. It identified the correct floor, the correct door. No one asked any questions. Apparently no one cared, even though the others in sight were wearing white lab jackets. Two women were busy with microscopes; several young men were talking to an older man, obviously a doctor. No one seemed to notice the quick search of the shelves high along the wall. The contents were conveniently labeled. It took only a few minutes to pour the powder, about two or three centigrams, from the sterile container into the small glass vial ready to receive it. That was at least ten times what was needed, more than enough. With the container recapped and replaced, with the vial pocketed, there was still no problem walking out, back now west on Cedar to York, north to Broadway and the car. The powder was known to be soluble in water.

The next day the Country Club Pharmacy in Whitneyville, a residential and shopping area north on Whitney Avenue several miles from Yale's Old Campus, displayed as usual on this holiday a variety of candy for Thanksgiving. Two boxes of chocolate-covered cherries, one on which to experiment if necessary, would do the trick. The teenage girl behind the front counter, deep in conversation on the telephone in her left hand, rang up the cash without a word. She was too preoccupied to notice, much less to recall, who had bought what.

At home after lunch, the powder mixed smoothly with sugar water. It dissolved to form a thin syrup. At hand lay a hypodermic needle left long ago among the belongings of a diabetic mother. It proved ideal for injecting each chocolate-dipped cherry with a little of the syrup. The needle left a visible mark on the outer surface of each candy, but it looked as if it were part of the intended design. More than half the syrup penetrated the candies, plenty to do the job. Carefully rewrapped in the silver paper in which each had come, the cherries looked delicious in their festive holiday box. An appropriate card completed the preparations. The beneficence was ready, but it wasn't what the witness was expecting.

It was an advantage to know something about the work habits of Yale employees. The personnel in the office of the secretary of the university would leave early, as usual, to beat the traffic for the Thanksgiving holiday. An anonymous call to the president's office confirmed that the building would be open until three for deliveries.

The anonymity of normal dress served as well as a disguise: a tan trench coat, a brown hat pulled down to hide the upper face, brown kidskin gloves. The rotunda off Hewitt Quadrangle at 2:45 that afternoon was empty of people. It took only a minute to saunter through the door into the court and look around to see if anyone was in the area. No one. A glance then at the windows of the president's office. No one visible, no one looking out. Then a brisk twenty yards to the door of Woodbridge Hall, into the building, left and quietly through the door to the suite of Celotto's offices. Another quick look around. Again no one in sight, though a mop leaning against the wall near the outer door suggested that a cleaning crew might be nearby. Tiptoe to the small office ahead, her redoubt. Put the package conspicuously on her desk. What was that sound? Perhaps a footfall. No, someone had bumped the mop while removing it. To be safe, wait a few minutes. Silence now. Quickly, quickly out of the suite, out of the building, still unobserved. Home in another five minutes. A cup of tea as a reward. Nothing further to do now but await developments.

As expected, nothing over the long Thanksgiving weekend. Yale was closed up tight. But on Monday again nothing happened. It was a day of anxiety. Waiting and waiting. Hourly news on the local radio station but not the anticipated report. A failed effort at diversion by driving to Westport for lunch. Tension and fatigue that night, no sleep.

Exhausted on arising Tuesday, but still no news on radio or TV. Nothing in the morning paper. What could have gone wrong? Powerful urge to inspect. First a cup of hot coffee. Then by car to the campus area, There was a parking space on High Street opposite the east side of the law school, along the west side of Hewitt Quadrangle. Around the corner on foot to Wall Street. Look left. Thank God! A police cordon in front of Woodbridge Hall. She must have taken the bait.

12.
DISCOVERIES

"What's this," Stavros had said, "an Old Blue Corpse?" Now Fawcett was on his way to inform President Stiles about the death, probably the murder, of Isabel Doughton, and Stavros was entering Woodbridge Hall where he had ordered a police cordon to block access to the building until he directed otherwise. Driving down from the Doughton house, his car's siren screaming, Stavros had planned his tactics for confronting Tony Celotto. The detective did not like dealing with Yale brass. They were generally aloof. They made him uneasy. He knew the Celotto family. He knew Tony put on no airs. But he wanted to take the offensive in his inquiries about Isabel Doughton, so he wanted to knock Tony off base, just a little, perhaps, but enough to show who was in charge. So playing it tough, he burst into the suite of the secretary of the university. "I want to see Miss Doughton, right away," he demanded of the receptionist.

"She's not in today."

"Then where the hell is she?" Stavros growled, loudly enough to be heard anywhere nearby.

Before the receptionist could reply, Tony Celotto came hurrying out of his inner office. "What's going on here?" he asked. Then, seeing Stavros, he continued, "See here, Stavros, you have no right to come in here shouting at my people. What do you think you're doing?"

"Trying to get your attention," Stavros replied. "It seems to take a lot to do that. Have you any idea where Miss Doughton is? Have you

155

tried calling her or don't you bother to find out what's up when people don't report for work?"

"I assume she's home sick," Tony answered, "but if you have any further questions, you had better improve your manners before you can expect any reply. You know better than to act like this. What's eating you, Stavros? If I report your behavior to the mayor, there'll be trouble."

"Trouble you've already got," Stavros said. "You never asked, did you, whether Miss Doughton was at home? I was just there. I had her taken away. She's been dead a few days, but no one at the university seems to have known or cared."

The receptionist let out a startled squeak. Tony looked incredulous. "Come into my office," he said after a brief silence. "We can talk there."

"Do you want some coffee?" Tony asked as the detective sat down next to his desk. Stavros shook his head and Tony continued, "You have to realize this news is a shock. Miss Doughton had been working in this office years before I got here. She was something of a fixture at Yale, and a law unto herself. She was a hard worker and a good one, so I let her come and go as she pleased. It never occurred to me to inquire about her absence. I trusted her judgment about her schedule. I just assumed she had a cold or had lingered away somewhere on the long weekend. If she had not come in by tomorrow, I suppose one of the staff would have been in touch with her. But she had no particular friends. She was a loner."

"She had at least one enemy," Stavros said. "Someone seems to have poisoned her. Got any ideas?"

"Poisoned? Poisoned! No, no, I've no ideas. Why should I have? I knew her only as an employee. I must admit no one liked her. She was snotty, made a fuss about her father having been a professor, as if there weren't plenty of professors' daughters. She ran this office like a marine boot camp. Didn't hesitate to tell off faculty who leaned on her. She ate too much, sort of greedy about her chocolates, always with her but never shared. Miss Doughton was not a nice person, but she was a top-notch executive secretary. I found her difficult, but I relied on her. I'm shocked and sorry that she's dead. What else can I say?"

"You always call her by her last name?" Stavros asked.

"Rarely. But no one I know regularly used her first name," Tony said, "probably not even her mother. Listen, Stavros, before you go any further, have you informed the president and Chief Fawcett?"

"Yeah, Fawcett was at the house. He'll be here any minute. He's going to spread the word. Right now, you can't see it, but we're putting men across the front of the building. I want everyone in this whole office out, but somewhere in the building until we can talk to them. I want no one coming in except Fawcett. And my men are going to sweep this place, especially Miss Doughton's space. So you tell them all, okay? Or would you rather have me do it my way?" Stavros grinned as he asked the last question.

"Lighten up and cut out the tough cop routine," Tony said. "I don't buy it. You think there was a murder so you're coming on strong, too strong. Leave my staff to me. I'll go up with them to the corporation room on the second floor. Don't keep us long if you expect us to wait. The women will be upset, and I want them to be able to go home."

"We'll be done with them in less than an hour," Stavros said. "Can you lend me a room for questioning?"

"Use my assistant's, under the stairs at the other side of the hall," Tony said, "I'm going to try to see President Stiles once everyone is upstairs, so you'll find me there if you need me."

While two city detectives were combing Isabel Doughton's little office, hardly more than a cubicle, for any evidence, however small or remote, Fawcett arrived at Woodbridge Hall to meet Stavros. "See here," Stavros said, "my men tell me there's a vault near Doughton's office. Did you keep that collar there? No more secrets, Chief. We're into a murder now. So tell me about what you're doing about the collar and who's involved."

"We're stuck, if you must know," Fawcett said. "And I've two professors working with me, Gerald Walsh from history and Lilith

Furman from the law school. He's close to President Stiles. She used to be a public defender in Boston. They were there when the collar was stolen."

"Better get them to meet us," Stavros said. "Today. I used to see Walsh play hockey. Quick little monkey he was."

That afternoon at 2:15 the four met. Stavros reviewed the events of the early morning and began to report about what his men had since found. "No prints in her office," he said, "except hers and other members of Celotto's staff. Desk had nothing very interesting in it except a half empty carton of Oreo cookies and some wrapping paper. Otherwise the usual stuff in the drawers—some Kleenex, nail file, scissors, paper clips, pencils, office junk. Top of her desk empty and table next to it empty, too, except for the computer on it."

"We'll need her code to access her files," Lilith said. "We'll have to find out whether anyone in the office knows the code. Maybe Tony Celotto does."

"Hey," Stavros said, "all that stuff is past me. How about you ask around for me, Miss Furman. Then if you find out, can you use the machine?"

"Oh, yes," Lilith said, "once I know the code. I'll be glad to try. And there's one more matter to explore, Detective Stavros. Isabel Doughton was in Tony Celotto's office on the evening when the president's collar was stolen."

"You better fill me in about the theft," Stavros said. "As I told Fawcett, this is a murder investigation."

Chief Fawcett told him the whole story. Tony Celotto or Dean Humber or Professor Barnard could easily have stolen the collar, he pointed out. They were all at the desk where it was lying. He admitted that they had no clue about the whereabouts of the collar or about who might have taken it except for those in the room when it was stolen. "And we've interrogated them and found nothing," Fawcett said. "At my request and President Stiles', Professor Walsh and Miss Furman are helping, but about all we've done recently is listen and wait."

"I'm taking over the grilling, then," Stavros said. "I want to hear their stories for myself. I'll see them all as soon as I can. Meanwhile we'll find out more about Doughton's personal life. And Miss Furman, you'll see about the computer, I hope. Professor Walsh, how about you come with me and Fawcett now to Celotto's office where you can give me your version of the party where the collar was taken? Thanks to you all. I'll fix it with Fawcett so we get together later. Keep in touch with him if you learn anything."

After Jerry gave Stavros a full account of the events as they had transpired in Tony Celotto's office on the evening the collar was stolen, Stavros and two of his men questioned Tony and his staff about the personal habits of Isabel Doughton. "We're going to have to talk to all those people again," Stavros told Fawcett over a cup of coffee at the Greek's on York Street. "But you know, I get the feeling that the women in that office don't know a damn thing about Doughton or her life. They were all scared of her, as far as I can see, probably too scared to try anything dangerous like poison. And they all say they spent the time from Wednesday afternoon to yesterday living it up for the Thanksgiving weekend. They think seeing their children all that time, or visiting their families, or having their mothers here for a few days is living it up. Bunch of old biddies, even the young ones. But the hell of it is that they have family witnesses for about every minute of the whole damned weekend. So that leaves me for now looking at Celotto and the others you and Walsh say were nearby when someone hooked that collar. What do you think, Chief?"

"I suspect you're right," Fawcett said. "Those women from the secretary's office aren't your types, Stavros, but they're not the types who murder their boss, either. Still, so far we're stumped about the theft. I've got nothing out of the people who were there."

The two sipped their coffee in silence for a few moments. "Okay," Stavros then said. "How about I give a few of the faculty types something to think about. I'll lean on them one by one. Question is, where to begin?"

"Walsh and Miss Furman and I," Fawcett replied, "think the only ones who could have snitched the collar without being seen by the others were the three standing around Celotto's desk. Celotto was there and Professor Barnard and Dean Humber. But as I told you, we've come up dry with all of them."

"I'll have a go at them," Stavros said. "First I want to find out more about them. So what do you say we go over now to Miss Furman's office and call Walsh to join us there. It's not yet five o'clock." They finished their coffees and left.

Jerry Walsh and Lilith Furman were talking when the chief and Stavros appeared. Stavros reported the conversation he had just had with Fawcett. "So," he concluded, "I'm going to give those three a hard time, but first I want you to explain what you were all doing at Celotto's office that evening and why in hell anyone there would have risked stealing that collar. Also which of them had dealings with Doughton?"

"I'll tell you what I know," Jerry said, "provided you keep it to yourself unless and until you're sure some of it has to do with the poisoning. And even then you say as little as possible. Is that agreeable? You see, confidential university affairs are involved."

"Jesus, Professor Walsh," Stavros replied, "we got a murder here. You got to tell the police everything you know about the case. I don't give a shit about Yale business. Who the hell does? But keep your shirt on. I won't say anything about anything except what I need to make an arrest when I'm ready."

"Well," Jerry said, "I admit that a lot of the story has already been in the papers, so you might as well hear it right." He then went on for half an hour, with occasional comments from Lilith, about the search for a new president, the membership of the faculty advisory committee, the candidates on the short list, and the decision to invite Shapiro. The meeting in Celotto's office, he explained, took place before Shapiro declined the offer he had received.

"So those three guys," Stavros said, after thinking about Jerry's account, "all wanted the job, right? Celotto and Barnard and Humber, right? And they were all there, at that desk, able to snatch the collar, right? So who took it? And which of them, if it was one of them, wanted to get rid of Doughton? The collar may have had nothing to do with

Doughton. That's the big question, right?"

"It sure is one big question," Fawcett said.

"So here's what I think," Stavros said. "My men will have another go at the women in Celotto's office and get to Doughton's neighbors. I'll take on our three wannabe presidents tomorrow. Fawcett, will you set that up for me? And Professor Furman, will you get at that computer stuff? Professor Walsh, you help her if you can, and you think about Celotto and Barnard and Humber. What kind of men are they? Who could steal? Who could kill? Don't talk to them. Leave that to me. But you know them. I don't. So you think about them, and I'll ask you what you think when I've seen them all."

Everyone agreed to those assignments, and Stavros and Fawcett left. But Jerry remained to compare impressions with Lilith.

Shocked though he was by the news of the death of Isabel Doughton, Arthur Stiles could not on that account rearrange his busy schedule. There was, in any case, no one with whom to commiserate, as Tony Celotto had assured him. So he was ready, as planned, for a private conference with Richard Mason, his former provost, at 2:30 that afternoon. The King had arranged that meeting at the urging of Proxmire Young who was sure that Arthur Stiles, and only he, would persuade Mason to take a positive view about becoming president of the university. Young, for his part, had sounded out the corporation search committee, which was eager to ask Mason provided that he would not decline out of hand. The Fellows, still smarting from Shapiro's decision, did not want to risk another disappointment, or to let the world learn that Yale had twice been refused. The King was not to offer Mason the position. Rather, he was to solicit Mason's promise to give an offer serious consideration.

For his part, Dick Mason made the appointment with the King with full knowledge of the agenda he would face, for Arthur Stiles, characteristically, had been wholly open about his intentions in requesting an hour or more with his friend and long-time associate. So Mason was equally open in his first remark as he entered the president's study. "Here I am, Arthur, ready to be brainwashed but resolved not to yield."

"I have no intention of brainwashing you," the King replied. "On the contrary, I asked you to see me because I'm interested in what you think about the logical next step in the presidential search. After all, no one on the faculty knows Yale better than you do, and no one else has your informed but distant view of recent developments."

"If you're referring to Dr. Shapiro's decision," Dick said, "I really know only what I've read in the papers. That's enough, I guess, unless he had some reason for declining that I haven't heard."

"To the best of my knowledge, he did not," the King said. "Still, it was a blow to the Fellows' hopes and Yale's prestige. I must say that the theft of the collar and today's news about Isabel Doughton's death haven't helped."

"Isabel Doughton? The fat woman in Tony's office?" Dick asked, surprised.

"Oh, you haven't heard? Let me tell you what Tony told me," the King said as he began to inform Mason.

"My God!" Dick said as Arthur Stiles completed his account. "Poison! You are absolutely right, that won't help our PR."

"Dick, you and I care about this place," the King said. "So we can agree that in the circumstances, an early decision about the next president would be helpful. But how do you feel about what remains of the Fellows' short list? That is, in case you don't know, Gene Barnard and Tony Celotto."

"They had better renew their search," Mason said.

"Prox Young is in a big hurry, and you can see why. So how about Barnard and Celotto?"

"Nice guys," Dick replied, "hard workers, loyal Blues, but short on distinction and discernment. I like them both, but Tony really knows too little about most of the academic enterprise, and Gene is flashy, funny, and narrow. They have to find someone else."

"Exactly what I told Proxmire Young," Arthur Stiles said. "And he agrees. That's why he and his committee want you to think seriously about becoming president. Furthermore, I think they're right."

"Arthur," Dick said, "There must be better qualified people."

"Probably there are," the King said, "but not on this faculty. And anyhow, they seem to want you. And you agree that time is a factor. Now I'm not going to pressure you. But I would like to know, if you're willing to tell me, why you won't at least think it over."

"Look, Arthur," Dick replied, "I'm flattered. But I really have had it with budgets and all that goes with them. Those years as provost persuaded me it was time for something else. And I don't like raising money. There's going to have to be a lot of that. No, I don't want the job."

"May I say," the King asked, "that it's the provost who has to work so hard on the budget. The president really gets involved only with the big picture, not the details, as you very well know. So if you were president, you could hand over the dirt work to your provost. I did. I handed it to you. What's more, in spite of your protest, you're good at raising money. You were the most successful class agent for three years running."

"I had a lot of help."

"You would have more as president," Arthur went on. "You could appoint your own director of development and help him select staff. Have you ever talked about the presidency with Martha? I'll bet she'd like to see you take it."

"No," Dick said. "She never interferes in my professional decisions, and I haven't broached the subject."

"Well, I suggest you do," the King said. "She'd be great at 43 Hillhouse, and your children are old enough to allow her the time."

"Your kind of brainwashing is almost painless," Dick said. "I confess that this leave of absence has been less satisfying than I had hoped it would be. I'm a bit restless. And you're right. I care a great deal about Yale. I'll talk to Martha. She knows me better than I know myself. I'll let you know what develops. But don't count on anything, and don't yet tell Young what I've told you."

"That's great," Arthur replied. "You understand, I'm not offering you the job. I'm authorized only to ask you to give it your most earnest thought. So your answer is exactly what I had hoped it would be. I'm delighted, and I thank you for your time. I once thought you were too private a man for the presidency, but this conversation has completed the change of mind I've been undergoing. So while you and Martha are weighing things, be sure she knows that I believe you are both precisely what Yale most needs right now."

"Thanks, Arthur, you have been more than kind," Dick said with characteristic understatement, shook the King's hand and left.

"What do you think about my assignment?" Jerry Walsh asked Lilith Furman after Stavros and Fawcett had left her office.

"It's easier than mine," Lilith replied. "I called the computer center while you were with Stavros and found that they have no record of Isabel Doughton's code word. Everyone is supposed to leave a confidential code with the supervisor there, but she apparently did not. So I have to ask Tony and all his staff, and if no one knows, as I suspect is the case, I'll have a major problem accessing her files."

"I'm sort of innocent about computers," Jerry said. "How does a code word work?"

"The code words go back to when we had computer terminals that were hooked into the mainframe at the computer building. The code words guarded confidential materials. Now with personal computers most users at Yale have retained their old code words which they need to access folders or their contents—their files and other documents stored in their computer hard disks." Lilith booted the computer on her desk and beckoned to Jerry to look over her shoulder. "See," she said, "it wants to know my code." Then, demonstrating, she typed "C-J-1-4-M." A list flashed on the screen of her computer monitor. The list consisted of a row of about twenty titles, each, as Lilith explained, a file containing documents on various subjects relating to her teaching. She typed the number of the line that said "Agency" and the first page of a lecture appeared on the screen. She hit another key and the pages of the lecture ran up the face of her monitor, stopping at the ninth page, the one she had asked for.

"Okay," Jerry said. "I can do most of that on my laptop, but I have no codes. Tell me, how did you get your code word?"

"I made it up," Lilith replied. "Any combination of letters and integers will do. My code word stands for 'Carter Jefferson is the one for me.' See, C-J-1-4-M. But that's confidential or some unauthorized person could break into my files."

"If no one knows Isabel's code," Jerry said, "it's going to be tough to figure it out."

"I'd have to be lucky," Lilith said. "There are, after all, 26 letters and ten integers, and I'm not a good enough mathematician to calculate the number of possible combinations. And I doubt I'll live long enough to try them all."

"I don't envy you," Jerry said. "I doubt Stavros realizes what a tough nut he handed you."

"As I said," Lilith replied, "your job is easier."

"So it is," Jerry said, "but if you have time, I'd like to gossip a little about it. See if you agree with my reading of the three men. Bob Humber obviously has a nasty streak. He seems to have gone out of his way to make an issue that would embarrass Yale. So I suppose he's mean enough to steal for the same purpose. Tony, as I read him, wouldn't dream of stealing, especially not something for which he is responsible. And I can't think what motive he could have had. Gene, in my opinion, wouldn't take the risk. He's ambitious. He wanted to be president, still does, for that matter. But if he were seen stealing, he'd blow it. No, if one of them stole the collar, I think it had to be Humber. But to be honest, I can't see any one of them as a murderer. Maybe there's no connection between the theft and the murder."

"I pretty much agree," Lilith said, "however, I'm going to bet there is a connection, but just now I don't believe any of the three had murder in him. But I'd modify your other points. Humber is not without principle. He really believes in the educational notions you and I find repugnant. So I doubt he intended to hurt Yale. He did it incidentally by going public to advance a cause that grabs him. If I'm right, that purpose does not reach to theft. I agree with you entirely about Tony, however. He's a sweetie and an innocent, or I can't read human nature. Now, I know you and Gene are great friends. But I don't trust him as much as you do. I think he's a conniver, anything for himself first. I believe he'd steal in a minute if it suited his purpose, but for the life of me I can't think of any purpose it could have suited. I've been thinking about all of them since the theft, and I admit I'm stuck."

"Thanks anyhow for sharing your thoughts," Jerry said. "I'm worried but still can't agree with you about Gene. I'll think it all over before we have to see Stavros again. Now I had better start for home. It's late and it's been a long day. I'm glad you're on my side, pal."

"We have our discoveries yet to make," Lilith said. "Don't lose any sleep over the problem. We need either some hard data or a brilliant hunch, probably both, and we can't force either. See you soon. And don't worry. I won't change sides unless you do."

13.
CONUNDRUM

The days that followed dragged for those investigating the poisoning of Isabel Doughton. On Thursday Stavros questioned Barnard, Celotto and Humber, but he learned nothing about the theft of the collar or the murder of Doughton. Lilith talked with all of the women in Tony's office, but neither they nor Tony himself knew the code word for Isabel Doughton's files. On Thursday and Friday two city detectives quizzed Doughton's neighbors. They learned that no one liked her. She had indeed been a busybody, and the couple who lived next door to her house were still angry with her for slitting open and reading mail that the post office had mistakenly delivered while they were away the previous summer. She had admitted her nosiness when they confronted her. But no neighbor had any apparent reason for killing her.

The following Monday brought the first break in the case. That morning the results of the autopsy at last reached Stavros. "We're still puzzled about the poison," Dr. Sol Cohen reported from the morgue, "but in her stomach we've found a trace of a strange substance we're looking into. She must have been eating some chocolate candy shortly before she died. The substance was in the candy. Chocolate covered cherries. I've got a couple of Yale professors, a pathologist and a pharmacologist, coming by any minute now. Maybe they can help us identify the poison. I've never run across it before."

"Call me back as soon as you know," Stavros said. "I'm going to go up to the university after I hear from you and talk to Fawcett. We've got to get a break. The damned case just isn't moving."

An hour later Dr. Cohen called back. "Wait until I tell you," he said to Stavros. "The poison is something quite new. The pharmacologist identified it almost as soon as he saw it. The Yalies are experimenting with it at the medical school. It's called tetrodoxin, or TTX. Pretty easy to come by from medical suppliers, they say, if you know what to ask for, and available in powder. They have a damn ton of the stuff at Yale, right out in the open in some of the medical labs. It works fast. Someone swallows a little, he's dead inside half an hour or an hour. Doesn't take much, maybe a couple of milligrams. Nasty stuff, too. Causes weakness, then frank paralysis, then respiratory compromise, and the victim knows it's working until he dies. She took it, in the chocolates obviously. Now you have to find out who put it there. I'm calling the coroner as soon as we hang up."

Stavros then called Fawcett. They agreed to ask Jerry Walsh and Lilith Furman to meet with them right after lunch. "We need to learn who the hell knew about this stuff," Stavros said, "and who was able to get hold of it. That should tell us a lot about the guys we suspect."

But that afternoon proved to be less useful than Stavros had hoped. He gave a full report to the others and asked the important questions. "So one of your three," Stavros concluded, "must have had the information and the means to snitch the poison. Which?"

Jerry waited a few seconds before responding. "This is less helpful than you could have known," he said. "During the last few years several important papers about TTX have received a big play even in the Yale weekly bulletin. So just about anyone in the Yale community could have known something about it, though maybe not enough to know where to get it. Still, the King was so proud of the research that he had Tony Celotto take the whole faculty advisory committee down to the lab where they had done the work. I was there, and Lilith, and Tony of course. We saw TTX. Gene Barnard is on the biological sciences divisional committee, and that committee has visited the same lab. Humber reads the bulletin and he knows his neighbors, one of whom was a lead investigator in the research. He also knows Dean

Montefiore who's been boasting about TTX to anyone who'll listen. So where are we? Right where we've been since the beginning, not even sure about any relationship between the collar and the murder, or about either and the poison."

"Shit," said Stavros, turning at once toward Lilith and adding, "I'm sorry. Forgot you were here."

"I've heard the word before," Lilith said.

"Have you got anywhere with the computer?" Stavros asked.

"Nope. Thus far a brick wall," Lilith replied. "Jerry and I were planning to compare hunches about a code word but we haven't yet had time."

"What I'm going to do," Stavros said, "is lean on those guys again but now about what they know about TTX and where to find it. So you and Professor Walsh do what you can about that code. My people have begun to try to trace the chocolate cherries, too. Maybe if we all stay with it, we'll get somewhere. What you say, Fawcett?"

"I think someone should talk to the doctors in that lab to see whether they have any ideas. And find out about security in the building. Could anyone just walk in?"

"Good," Stavros said. "You do that, will you? Better if you poke around than if my men or I do. Now, all of you remember, what I've told you is classified. We're not going public about the poison until we're ready. The doctors agreed to that. So keep your mouths shut."

They all nodded and the meeting broke up.

"Get me Freeman and Jensen," Stavros barked at the duty officer at police headquarters as soon as he returned. "If they're out, get on the horn and have them come back now." He banged the door to his small office as he entered it, sat down at his desk, and for the tenth time went over the report that Detectives Peter Freeman and Joan Jensen had given him after they had swept Isabel Doughton's house. As he had recalled, they had found nothing of importance. Only her prints and those of her cleaning woman. An empty tea cup. A kettle, burned out, on the stove. House neat as a pin, and nothing in the least unusual.

His people had come up empty in Doughton's office, too, though it was now clear that the wrapping paper in the desk had probably been for the chocolates. The autopsy report had reminded him that somewhere there had to be the box the chocolates had come in. Probably at the house, but Freeman and Jensen had not found it.

His thinking had reached that point when the two detectives knocked and came in. "Where the hell you been, sleeping it off?" Stavros asked, greeting them with his customary brand of cordiality and letting out some of his frustration.

"Hey, Stavros, we were next door. We came as soon as the desk told us you wanted us," Jensen replied. "So lay off." She was a woman who took no guff from anyone, not even Stavros of whom most of the other detectives were at least a little afraid.

"Okay, so you're a hero," Stavros said. "But maybe a blind hero— you, too, Freeman. You were supposed to go over Doughton's house like you were looking for treasure. You found nothing. But there's got to be a box there that had chocolate-covered cherries in it. So now, goddammit, go on back and find it. Don't even answer me. Go! And bring the box back."

They went. "He's sure as hell got a hair up today," Freeman said as he got into the police cruiser that Jensen was waiting to drive. "We better find the damn box."

They did, but not until they had been looking for more than an hour. It had been dropped, it appeared, behind the stove, out of sight unless you were on your knees looking under the stove toward the back well. Later Stavros theorized that Doughton had dropped it when she put the kettle on. It had only her prints on it. When they found it, Freeman and Jensen did not pause to theorize. They just rushed the box back to headquarters.

The label on the box, "Georg Tremain, 12 rue de le Monde, Paris," spurred Stavros to his next move. He had the desk put out a call for patrolman Henri Labrecque, the only French-Canadian on the force. Labrecque, who was off duty, did not call in until almost five o'clock. As he then reminded Stavros, who wanted him to come in and call Paris for him, for Stavros knew no French, it was too late in Paris for a chocolate store to be open.

So it was Tuesday morning before Stavros, with Labrecque translating, talked to the proprietor of "George Tremain," the merchant whose name the store bore. From him Stavros learned that a New York importer, Driscoll and Son Inc., with an office on South William Street in downtown Manhattan, handled all the candy Tremain exported to the United States. Still on the telephone, Stavros discovered from the accountant at Driscoll Inc. that all the chocolate the company imported went directly from the docks at Hoboken to jobbers in various parts of the country. The jobber serving New Haven and its vicinity, McNulty Confections, was located off Interstate 91 in North Haven, Connecticut, not far from police headquarters.

Stavros had Jensen and Freeman on their way to that address before the morning reached ten o'clock. They were to get a list of all retailers in the New Haven area who stocked the chocolate-covered cherries. They were then to visit every store they identified to see whether they could find out from any clerk who remembered just who had bought Tremain cherries. The candy was expensive, so someone might just recall the sale.

"The goddamn list is so long," Jensen complained when the two detectives returned, "that we could retire before we get to all the stores. How do you want us to proceed? By town? By alphabet?"

"The victim worked at Yale," Stavros replied. "Whoever poisoned her probably does too. So begin around the university and in places where the Yalies shop. Then if you don't get lucky, go round in circles barking. What you want me to do, think for you?"

"It's still going to take a long time," Jensen, resigned but surly, told Freeman as they set about their task. "That Stavros pisses me off. He swears at women officers but never at you. Goddamn pig!"

"Ah, stop fussing," Freeman replied. "I count only five places near here that the local Yalies are likely to go into. Sure, dozen others in the fancy suburbs—Woodbridge and Guilford and like that—but let's get started with the five and see what we get. That may shut up Stavros for now. He's got a copy of the list. Maybe he'll send someone else to the sticks. You want to drive? Let's go, then, Yale Bookstore first."

That Tuesday afternoon Harry Grayson, outgoing managing editor of the *Yale Daily News,* was also busy investigating leads he had come across. Harry still hoped for the big scoop that had eluded him for so long. Now it seemed close to hand. On a fortuitous Sunday, returning to New Haven from New York where he had spent a lively weekend, Harry had eaten a quick lunch in a coffee shop on Lexington Avenue near Grand Central Station. A couple sitting at the counter there caught his attention. As they left their places, he suddenly realized why they seemed familiar. The man was Dr. Aaron Shapiro whose photograph had appeared on the front page of the *Yale Daily* when he was thought to be the university's next president. The quite beautiful woman with him who had been hanging on his every word also looked familiar.

Only after she had gone did Harry place her as the wife of a faculty member. Except the woman he remembered had sort of gray hair, while the one he had just seen was blond. He had seen her with her husband a year or more ago at some Yale event, probably, to the best of his memory, a football game. Harry remembered beautiful women. He had always wanted one himself. That fantasy beguiled him until he boarded his train for New Haven. Just after a stop at 125th Street, as he was dozing off, it came to him. The woman he had seen had to be the same woman for whom Shapiro had given up the Yale presidency. And no one had used her name. Now Harry thought she was Eugene Barnard's wife, if his memory was correct. If he could be sure, he would be on to a possible scandal that could shake the small world in which he lived.

The following Saturday, indifferent to his pending final exams, Harry borrowed his roommate's car and drove to Viney Medical University in Yonkers. There he talked to everyone who was willing to answer his questions. A young doctor, who said he knew who Shapiro was but had never met him, retailed a rumor current at the university to the effect that Shapiro was having an affair with a married woman who lived in Stamford. Next Harry drove to Dobbs Ferry to locate Shapiro's residence. The teenager raking the last leaves from the lawn proved not to be one of Shapiro's sons, but he had met a pretty woman who was at the house that morning before she went off with the family for the day. They had been introduced. As he recalled, her name was Strafford.

Sunday Harry called Stamford information to inquire about the phone number of a Miss or Mrs. Strafford. There were two interesting possibilities—an E. Strafford and a Charlene Strafford. Next Harry drove to Stamford. The address for Charlene Strafford, which he tried first, proved to be in a rather impoverished area where most of the people on the streets were Latinos or blacks. Harry tried the other address. His luck held. Emerging from the condominium where Harry had just parked, Aaron Shapiro walked right past Harry's car.

Harry pressed on. He entered the lobby, found a calling card for Elizabeth Strafford over a bell there, rang the bell, and was buzzed to enter. The door to the unit where Elizabeth Stafford lived was open when Harry got there. He knocked.

"What did you forget this time, darling?" a voice called out.

"I guess I'm not who you expected," Harry answered.

Seconds later the beautiful blond came to the door wearing a warm-up suit. "Just who are you?" she asked when she saw Harry. "What do you think you're doing here?"

"I'm Harry Grayson from the *Yale Daily News*, and I was about to ask you the same questions," Harry replied.

"Oh, Lord," the woman said. "I suppose I have to face a nosy Newsie sooner or later. Come on in. How did you find me?"

Harry told her. She swore him to write nothing until after he had talked to Dr. Shapiro, in return for which she promised to arrange an appointment with him. Then she told Harry that she was indeed a faculty wife, but in the process of getting a divorce from Gene Barnard. Harry gasped. "But now we at the *News* think Professor Barnard will be the next president," he said.

"I suppose that would be some kind of poetic justice," she said. "I hadn't intended to do him a favor. Now young man, you run along. Remember your promise. I'll call you at the *News* tomorrow evening to tell you when and where my fiancé will meet you. Until you've talked to him, not one word or I'll report you to the police for entering a private building on false pretenses. Go along. I was planning to jog and I want to get started."

After Harry left Betty took a deep breath. She had said that Aaron was her fiancé, she realized. Well, she did love him. Time to get rid of her hang-ups. She gave Aaron time to drive home and then phoned him. "Hi, love," Betty said. "If you still want to marry me, I accept."

"Name the day!" he almost shouted.

Betty then told him about young Grayson. "So he brought me to my senses," she concluded, "but now he wants to see you."

Monday evening she called Grayson to set an appointment for him at Aaron's office at three the next day. So on Tuesday afternoon Harry drove back to Yonkers.

"I've been expecting you, Mr. Grayson," Shapiro said when his secretary showed Harry in. "You have violated my privacy and the privacy of my fiancée, and I don't like it. But since you know as much as you do, I'm going to tell you the whole story under certain conditions. Now sit down and let me explain." Harry sat.

"First," Shapiro continued, "I have this tape recorder running so that I'll have a record of everything we say. If you do not report our conversation accurately, I'll release the tape to the *New York Times* and make you and the *Yale News* look silly. If you won't proceed that way, you may leave. Second, you are not in any way to imply that there is scandal here because there is none. I met Ms. Strafford and fell in love with her before I knew she was Mrs. Barnard. Strafford is her professional name, and we met at a professional conference. Get that straight. Finally, I will answer no questions. I'll say what I have to say, and then you will leave. Are you willing to proceed?"

"Yes, sir," Harry replied, though he had not expected so inflexible an interview. Dr. Shapiro, he thought to himself, was as firm as his own father. Shapiro would have enjoyed knowing Harry's feelings. He had meant to be strictly paternal.

"Well then," Shapiro went on, "this won't take long. Mrs. Barnard fell in love with me. So we became engaged to be married. I repeat, there is no scandal there. I'm a widower. She's getting a divorce. As soon as she's free, we will be married. We are both adults. But I did not know her feelings about Yale until I had agreed to become the university's president. I had not inquired, which I should have done. She had not volunteered, though I wish she had. Only after I had agreed to take the offer did she tell me that living in New Haven as the wife of the president was not something she would be able to do. I love her. I intend to live with her. So I told Mr. Proxmire Young that I had after all to decline his offer. I had hoped to protect Ms. Strafford's privacy. You broke in. I consider you a brash young man. That's the whole story. Be sure to get it right. Now you may go."

Harry left. Shapiro at once called Proxmire Young and told him exactly what had happened. Young was annoyed but not upset. As he said, the news damaged Shapiro, Betty Barnard and perhaps Gene Barnard, but not the university. At Shapiro's request, Young agreed to inform Arthur Stiles.

Shapiro's conditions and his irritation had not dimmed Harry Grayson's high spirits. He drove back to New Haven in a celebratory mood. The story, even as he had promised to write it, would still make a big splash. But he had not liked being called brash. The word, in his interpretation, implied immaturity and irresponsibility. He decided to prove he was adult himself by calling Professor Barnard to tell him what the *News* would publish before he saw the story in print.

That evening Gene Barnard had just returned to his house after a squash game when the phone rang. It was Harry Grayson who reported exactly as he had planned to. Terse and noncommittal in his response, Gene hung up as soon as Harry finished. But he was churning inside.

At once he called Sylvia Wheatley, as he did every day. "Darling, wait until you hear this," Gene said, and he told her all he had just learned. "You know," he continued, "I lost all interest in Betty's amours once you and I found we loved each other. So I didn't give a damn that she was sleeping with Shapiro or anyone else. The bitch must have hated helping my cause. Let the *News* run off at the mouth. It won't hurt us. But how I do miss seeing you."

"Gene, dear," Sylvia said, "there really isn't any reason why we can't see each other in New Haven just as long as no one knows. I've missed you so much. And I've been thinking about it. It gets dark early now. Why can't you bundle up in your overcoat and a hat and scarf and come over here for a late dinner tonight and every other night you're free? No one will know. You can stay as long as it's dark, all night, until almost eight in the morning. And we will both sleep better if we're together. I need you here."

"Sylvia," Gene said, "you're absolutely right. Young Grayson told me that Shapiro told him there was no scandal in a widower loving a woman in the process of getting a divorce. Well, there is no scandal in a widow loving a man in the same circumstance. I just need to be very discreet until the Fellows make up their minds. Betty got Shapiro out of the way. She also set a wonderful precedent for us. We'll wait for the dark, as you suggest, but we'll be together. I'll be there tonight as soon as I've changed clothes."

"You could even leave your clothes behind," Sylvia said, laughing.

That afternoon detection proved to be easier for Harry Grayson than for Freeman and Jensen. The two detectives reached the Yale Bookstore on Broadway a long block west of York Street with Jensen still in a snit about Stavros. "Listen," Freeman told her, "the way you feel, better let me do the talking or you'll bite someone."

"Bite you if you don't shut up," Jensen replied, but she was just as glad to leave the questioning to her partner. She followed Freeman into the east entrance and up to a counter near where boxes of candy were on display. "There they are," she said, pointing to a stack of some seven boxes of Georg Tremain chocolate-covered cherries. Freeman picked up a box and looked at the price. "Holy Moses!" he said, handing the box to Jensen. "Can you believe this price? Must be made of gold." Jensen shook her head. $15.75 struck her as too much for twelve candies.

"May I help you?" a woman in a blue cotton jacket asked.

"We're detectives," Freeman said, displaying his badge, "and we're here to ask some questions about these candies. You the manager?"

"I am of this section," she replied. "I'm Doris Flagg. What do you want to know?

"We would like to find out," Freeman said, "if you can tell us who bought this kind of chocolate candy in the weeks before Thanksgiving."

"You must be kidding," Doris Flagg said. "How could I know? We bought half a gross of those you're holding for delivery about November 10, for the holidays, Thanksgiving and Christmas. Probably have about thirty boxes left here and in the storeroom. I could check if you want. But we have no record of who bought the boxes we sold. The customer takes a box to checkout over there. The girl at the register punches in the number of the item for inventory control, takes the cash and makes change. If it's a charge we accept Visa and Master Card and Am Ex, and the girl punches in the card's number automatically when she checks the customer's credit. So I can give you a register tape and you can get a lot of credit card numbers from it, but if the purchase was for cash, I've no record that will help you. The numbers won't either unless you have access to all the credit card companies and their files so you can get names for each number, a big job. That's it. You can see the registers are busy even now. Days before Thanksgiving and Christmas this place is a madhouse."

"Maybe one of the clerks might remember?" Jensen asked.

"No way. The check out clerks don't know the customers. Mostly they don't even look at faces when they're busy. No, no way they'll remember."

"She's right," Freeman said to Jensen. "Nothing here for us. Thanks, Doris. Now let's get going. We've other stops to make." He put the box of chocolates back on the stack and started out, with Jensen in his wake.

"Where next?" Jensen asked as she slid into the driver's seat.

"Mama Celotto's deli, on Orange Street."

"I know where it is," Jensen snapped, still in a foul mood. "But it's not a deli. It's a fancy food store, Italian specialties, expensive."

"That's how come they carry candy that costs more than a buck a piece," Freeman said. "Step on it. It's getting late."

Jensen parked in the lot next to the store. "I'll do the talking this time," she said. "I been in here once or twice for frozen lasagna. She may remember me."

They found Mama Celotto at her register, talking to a customer whose purchases she was totaling. "Take some ginger," she was saying, opening a large jar at the counter. "It's good for you."

Jensen waited until the customer, who accepted a piece of candied ginger, had picked up her bags of groceries and left. "We're from the police, Mama," she then said to Mrs. Celotto—everyone called her Mama—"and we have some questions, but nothing to worry you. You may know my face. I come in for frozen pasta. Here's my badge. This guy's my partner."

"So ask," Mama said, obviously uncomfortable with detectives in her store.

"You sell Georg Tremain chocolate-covered cherries," Jensen said. "We want to know who bought them in the days before Thanksgiving."

"Who bought? I stocked three dozen boxes. Maybe a dozen left. Who bought two dozen boxes? What am I? A camera with a memory? Before the holiday we're very busy." Mama Celotto shrugged. "Sometime I am in the storeroom, sometime here, with extra help part of every day. How do I know who bought?"

"You talk to your customers," Freeman said. "Maybe you talked about the candy."

"Oh, sure, we gossip when the store's empty on a Tuesday. Mrs. Margolis, who just left, has a new granddaughter," Mama said. "No time for talk around Thanksgiving. Too much of a rush."

"So you can't remember?" Jensen said.

"Look, I don't know who bought the candy," Mama said impatiently. "How many times do I have to tell you? But I know who loves the cherries. My son Tony. He takes a box home whenever he thinks I'm not looking. I never let on. He's a good boy, does everything for his mother. I'm glad to know he eats."

"Thank you," Jensen said, glancing toward Freeman out of the corner of her eye. "You've helped us."

As they returned to their cruiser, she said, "Hold onto your hat, Freeman. When Stavros hears what we just did, he'll flip. Tony Celotto's office is where Doughton worked."

"Yeah, I got that," Freeman replied. "Doesn't prove a hell of a lot. You better drive up to the Orange Market, couple of blocks north. We'll check there before we go in. Then you can tell Stavros all about it. Time you sweetened him up."

But the proprietor at the Orange Market told them just about what Mama Celotto had. "Ain't anyone going to remember," Freeman said as they drove away. "Might as well leave the other places for tomorrow if Stavros wants us to continue this shit. Let's go in. You report. I have to get ready for tonight. We got a gig at a joint in Milford."

Back at headquarters Stavros did not flip when he heard the news. But he was privately pleased about the word on Tony Celotto. To Jensen he said, "So no one remembers. Okay. Enough for now. You and Freeman see me tomorrow before you go out. I want to do some thinking tonight. You done okay, Jensen. Keep it up."

Jensen was surprised at how much she welcomed a little praise.

Before leaving Lilith's office Monday, Jerry agreed to return the next afternoon to help her try to find Isabel Doughton's code word. In Isabel's office on Tuesday they began with a list Lilith had constructed of letters of the alphabet interspersed with numbers from zero to nine and arranged in groups of five. Two hours later they admitted to each other that they were stumped. "Good lord," Jerry said, stretching, "we could be at this for days with no results. It's a frustrating conundrum."

"We've got to try something else," Lilith said. "Did you think of anything about her last night that might give us a clue?"

"Karen and I talked about her for at least an hour," Jerry replied. "Karen used to see her now and then marketing at the Whitneyville Food Center, though they were scarcely pals. About all Karen could remember that was notable about her was her habit of ordering small amounts of meat. Drove the butcher crazy, Karen said, when Isabel asked for a quarter of a pound of ground sirloin, or two slices of cold roast beef, or a chicken leg. Apparently she never bought more than she intended to eat immediately. So Karen suggested that we try words like 'stingy' or 'mean,' but those don't have five letters."

"How about 'close'?" Lilith suggested, typing the word onto the computer. Nothing happened. "Wrong word," she said, "but at least it's an idea. What else can you think of?"

"What's a five letter word for fat?" Jerry asked.

"She wouldn't have called herself that," Lilith replied, but she typed "obese" just to see. No luck. "Who's good at Scrabble?" she asked.

"Gene is," Jerry said, "but we can scarcely ask him."

Just then the telephone rang. "Who could that be?" Lilith said, looking at her watch. "It's late, five fifteen, and I told Tony's secretaries I did not want to be disturbed."

To her surprise, it was Detective Stavros. "Any chance that Professor Walsh is with you?" he asked. "Fawcett said he might be, and so did his wife. I need to talk to you both."

"We're both here," Lilith said. "When do you want to see us?"

"I'll be right there if you'll wait," Stavros said. "I'm close, in Fawcett's office. I'll bring him along."

Lilith told Jerry that Stavros and Fawcett were on their way, and while waiting, they resumed their guessing without effect.

In less than ten minutes Stavros and Fawcett arrived at Woodbridge Hall. Stavros spoke out right away. "Here's the skinny," and he went on to report what Jensen had told him. "So I decided," he continued, "to talk to Fawcett who suggested talking to you. My people aren't going to get anywhere asking who bought candy. No one will remember. But one of you could ask around, casual-like, at two places on our list just to see what you might find. You know, ask about a friend, ask about Barnard or Humber. We know Celotto could get his hands on the candy. What about the other two? You could ask some kind of questions at the two local places that stock the cherries where my people haven't gone yet. Fawcett agrees. Either of you game?"

"I don't like the idea of Lilith exposing herself that way," Jerry said. "After all, one person has been killed."

"How about you?" Stavros asked.

"Sure," Jerry said, "if I know the stores that you want to have questioned. Otherwise I think I'd be spinning my wheels."

"Two drug stores," Stavros said. "Country Club Pharmacy in Whitneyville and Hall Benedict Pharmacy on Orange Street."

"The first is easy," Jerry said. "I shop there myself and we order our prescriptions from them. Fellow named Lester Brauer owns the place. He's a pharmacist himself, and I've known him for years. But I've never been in the other except to buy a stamp now and then. Why not handle that one yourself?"

"That's a done deal," Stavros said. "Can you try tomorrow?"

"Yes," Jerry said. "I'll let you know what I learn. I'm no help to Lilith anyhow. She can guess code words as well by herself as with me at her side."

After Stavros and Fawcett had departed, Lilith and Jerry started to their respective homes. "Hey, friend," Lilith said as Jerry let her out of his car, "don't advertise your mission. I wouldn't want anyone poisonous to be angry with you."

"Don't worry," Jerry replied. "And I do not intend to eat any chocolates either."

"You know," Lilith said, closing the car door, "first thing tomorrow I'm going to try 'candy' as a code word."

It was after six in the evening before Proxmire Young reached Arthur Stiles. The King had been at a development meeting all day. "Anything new on Mason?" Prox asked. "I confess that at the outset of this search I though Mason too much like you, too much the academic liberal for these times. I even said as much to Walsh. But as with so many things, so with Mason, I've changed my mind. The discussions about Shapiro persuaded me that the central questions we had to answer had to do with ability, experience and broad-mindedness, including enthusiasm for science as well as for the arts. We did need a man like you, and we'd be lucky to find one. Shapiro qualified on those counts. So emphatically does Mason. So I hope he's interested."

"He just called," the King said. "He talked it over with Martha, his wife, and she was all for his taking the job. She said he'd been studying non-profits for years and the presidency would be a kind of fulfillment. She told him that, with their children now out of grade school, she would welcome taking on the things Charlotte has done so well, though perhaps not as much in the garden. And after thinking about it, he decided she was right. So he's eager to be asked to serve."

"He'll be asked," Prox said. "The Fellows' committee has just about decided as much. I'll schedule a full Fellows' meeting before Christmas so that we can really celebrate. Until then, I guess we'd better keep a lid on the matter."

"I agree, but I'd like your permission to tell Jerry Walsh confidentially. He's been so much involved."

"Do that, Arthur," Prox said. "He knows how to keep his mouth shut. And tell him please how grateful I am for all his help. It was his committee that made the real case first for Shapiro and then for Mason. We might have come out the same way without them, but they took the lead."

"He'll be glad you feel that way," the King replied, saying goodbye.

14.
CLUES

As he reached his office Wednesday morning, Jerry Walsh was struck by the headline on the *Yale Daily News* at his door. Harry Grayson had written his story according to the guidelines Aaron Shapiro had laid down, but he had prefaced it with a tabloid's leader: "ADULTERESS FACULTY WIFE." "Damn," Jerry thought as he read Grayson's account. "How awful for Betty, and for Gene and Shapiro, too. And scarcely adultery at that! Talk about taste!" He called home to inform Karen, who was outraged. They agreed she would ask Gene to join them for cocktails and dinner, but otherwise they could think of nothing helpful, though Karen intended to try later to reach Betty at her office to express their regret about the publicity. As it worked out, Gene thanked Karen but said he was busy that evening, and Betty was in New York for the day on a tax case. More important for them both, the *News* story made no waves. No national newspaper picked it up. Except at Yale in this particular case, faculty adultery was no longer news. Harry Grayson had yet to achieve a major scoop that carried much beyond New Haven.

Busy with overdue correspondence, Jerry found it was almost noon before he reached the Country Club Pharmacy on the mission he had agreed to undertake for Stavros. He went at once to the rear counter to ask for the proprietor, Lester Brauer, who was also the senior pharmacist and manager. Jerry had known him casually for more than a decade. "Hello, Professor Walsh," Brauer greeted him as he emerged from behind his shelves of prescription medicines, "what can I do for you today?"

"Les," Jerry said, "if you're willing, I'd like to talk to you privately for a few minutes."

"Sure. Let's go into my office," Brauer said, leading the way to a small office off the rear corridor of the store, and closing the door after Jerry entered. He sat at his desk and motioned Jerry to take a straight-backed wooden chair near it.

"What's the matter?" Brauer then asked. "Nothing serious, I hope. Maybe a GU infection for which you need a prescription?"

"No, nothing like that," Jerry said. "I've come to you for some information about your customers. I won't repeat what you say, and I want to know nothing involving their medical history or their personal habits. If you will tell me, I want to find out only two things. First, whether several particular people do or do not regularly shop here."

"I'll be glad to tell you that," Brauer said. "It's not confidential anyhow. Who did you have in mind?"

"Three men who are at Yale. But first I need your promise not to repeat this conversation to anyone."

"You got it."

"Then they are Dean Robert Humber of the Law School, Tony Celotto, the secretary of the university, and Professor Eugene Barnard."

"Dean Humber is a good customer," Brauer said. "Tony I knew once at grammar school, but he comes in only now and then to get bath salts for his mother. The professor I guess I've heard of, but I don't know him. Wouldn't know him if I saw him."

"I see," Jerry said. "You carry Georg Tremain chocolate-covered cherries, don't you?"

"Yes. Good item for the holidays. We laid in three dozen boxes, maybe four."

"I don't suppose you or one of your sales people would know who bought any of them," Jerry said.

"I wouldn't, Brauer replied. "The candy counter is up front and I never work it. Someone might come back to the other counter to charge a box of candy, though, and then we'd have a record. I'd have to go through an awful lot of records to find out who charged candy, and even then, it wouldn't indicate what kind of candy. It would just list 'candy' and the amount of the charge."

"That won't be necessary," Jerry said, "at least not now. May I ask again if I change my mind?"

"Yeah. But then I'd trust you to go through the records yourself. I'm too busy. It's Christmas time! I'm up to my ears."

"I'll do that if I have to," Jerry said. "I'll let you know. Thanks for your help."

"You're welcome," Brauer said. "Before you go, why not buy some of those cherries yourself? They are very tasty."

"Thank you," Jerry said, "but not today. Just now I couldn't get one past my lips." He departed without explaining his remark, and Brauer never thought to ask.

Lilith Furman, feeling restless, nevertheless spent the morning in conferences with her students. After an early lunch, her mind on code words, she walked over to Isabel's office, started the computer, and typed in the word she had been so eager to try: C-A-N-D-Y. To her disappointment, nothing again. She had such a strong hunch that she could hardly believe it had misled her. For several minutes she sat still, reflecting about the problem. Her hunch would not go away. So she tried S-W-E-E-T. Still no luck. Still a powerful sense of being on the right track. Women's intuition, she mused, was perhaps just a male myth, or in her case, a male myth she had absorbed. She let words run through her mind. After a few more minutes she tried C-O-C-O-A. Once again the word did not call up Doughton's files.

At about two o'clock the telephone rang on Isabel's desk. Lilith picked it up. Stavros was calling, looking for Jerry. Stavros had drawn a blank at the Hall Benedict Pharmacy and wanted to know if Jerry had met with better luck. Lilith promised to call back if and when Jerry appeared. Stavros said he had just about concluded that the three men suspected in the theft had nothing to do with the poisoning. He was on his way to the medical school to join Fawcett in interrogations about TTX and its availability.

He had no sooner hung up than Jerry walked in. "Stavros is looking for you," Lilith said. "He wants to know what you found at the drug store."

"He'll wait," Jerry said. "I want first to talk to you." He then reported his conversation with Brauer, omitting nothing and stressing that the druggist did not know or even recognize Barnard.

"I don't see that that proves anything," Lilith said. "Humber could have bought candy at the front counter without charging it and without being recognized by the clerk. So could Tony Celotto. For that matter, any one of the three could have bought the candy at Mama Celotto's or the Yale Bookstore. I think tracing the candy leads only to a dead end."

"You're probably right," Jerry allowed, "but have you any better idea?"

"I have to admit I'm flunking on code words," Lilith replied, and she went on to recount the irrelevance of her hunches earlier in the day.

"I have a lot of respect for your hunches," Jerry said. "Why not try a few more? What can we lose?"

They played word games for five minutes when suddenly Lilith had another hunch. "How about S-N-O-O-P?" she asked. "She must have known her own reputation."

"Go ahead," Jerry said.

But the result remained worthless.

"Has it occurred to you," Jerry said, "that she might have used a childlike code? She acted rather like a child with her nosiness. Suppose she deliberately kept her code word a secret and, expecting someone to try to guess, wrapped her secret in another, easily remembered secret. For example, H-E-A-V-Y describes her, and she may have thought of that. We could try. But she might have predicted just that and switched H-E-A-V-Y to P-O-U-N-D."

"Sounds complicated," Lilith said, "but we might as well try both." She did. No useful result. "Still," Lilith then added, "I kind of like your game. Instead of S-N-O-O-P I'll try P-O K-E-Y." That, too, flunked the test.

"Don't give up," Jerry said. "It's just as good as playing games with random letters and numbers."

"Okay, you try."

"Maybe she liked puns," Jerry said. "They're sort of childish. Let's try your earlier words as puns."

"Well," Lilith said, "the first I think of for S-W-E-E-T is S-U-I-T-E." She typed the word, and to her amazement and Jerry's, the screen of the computer flashed on Isabel Doughton's list of files.

"Hallelujah!" Lilith cried.

Jerry, who had been leaning over her shoulder so as to read the screen, jumped up and flung his hands in the air. "Now don't call Stavros," he said as he descended. "Let's have a go on our own first."

On the screen of the computer Jerry saw an alphabetized list, obviously an index to Isabel Doughton's files. While he watched, Lilith ran the index up and down the screen to get a sense of how the material was organized. After she had gone through the index twice, at Jerry's suggestion she returned to the entry labeled "Yale University" under which Doughton had a number of subheads. The first read "Buildings and Grounds"; another "Campus Police"; still others followed until they came to "President" and the "President and Fellows."

"Let's try that one," Jerry said. Lilith used the mouse to retrieve the file in question. She began, in effect, to leaf through it. After some pages she came to a page labeled "Fellows Search Committee" which contained the minutes of the first of that committee's sessions, followed in sequential pages by further minutes.

"She knew everything that was going on!" Jerry exclaimed. "What do you make of that?"

"Tony had her type up the minutes he took," Lilith said. "I'll bet there are copies in his file or in Proxmire Young's. Young would have wanted the minutes, and Tony doesn't know how to type."

"Perfect arrangement for a snoop," Jerry said.

"I can't see that it mattered," Lilith said. "She was his confidential secretary, and she didn't gossip or she could not have kept that job."

"I hope you're right," Jerry said. "Let's keep going." Lilith found that the file stopped with the last of the minutes. She went back to the index again and began to run it up and down again. "I'm looking for something interesting," she said as she worked. "Any ideas?"

"What about the list under the word 'Personal,'" Jerry said. Lilith fixed that list on the screen.

"Hey, it's kind of code again," Jerry Observed. He read aloud the words in the alphabetical order in which they were listed: "MABOY, MOUND, MOUTH, PSYCH, ROMEO." One by one, Lilith put them each on the screen. To her surprise and Jerry's each was followed by one word only, the same word for them all: "MONEY."

"What now?" Jerry asked.

The telephone rang. It was Stavros again. "He just walked in," Lilith said. "I'll put him on." She did, and Jerry gave Stavros a brief account of his visit to the Country Club Pharmacy.

"So we both struck out," Stavros said. "Is your buddy getting anywhere with the computer?"

"She's full of frustrations," Jerry said, bidding Stavros goodbye.

"What did you mean by that?" Lilith asked.

"Well, I was talking about you, and you are," Jerry said. "It's Wednesday, so you miss Carter. We're not solving much yet. Stavros asked how you were getting along, and I didn't want to lie to him."

"Not funny," Lilith said. "We should tell him the literal truth."

"I don't want to tell him more than we have to about the presidential search. That's why I want us to stay loose and proceed without him until we find something he should know. Okay?"

"I see your point," Lilith said. "We'll do it your way for now, though I'm uncertain about our next step."

"What do you make of 'MONEY'?" Jerry asked.

"Let's go back to the main index," she said, and began again to scroll. They sat and looked for some time.

"It's half past four," Jerry said. "My eyes and back are killing me. Let's try some entry, any entry, but hold the scrolling."

"I'll go to 'Yale University,'" Lilith said, doing so and starting along the subheads. "Here's one we haven't examined. 'Secretary's

Office.' Look. It has several entries. 'Secretary's Office-Budget' and 'Secretary's Office-Furnishings' and so on to 'Secretary's Office- Personnel' and here's 'Secretary's Office-Petty Cash.' She certainly was an organized woman!"

"Petty cash is money," Jerry said, yawning.

"I'll call it up," Lilith said as there was a knock on the door. It was one of the secretaries, announcing that she was leaving early for a doctor's appointment. "By all means, Alice," Lilith said. "Before you go, please put the phone on the answering machine. I don't want to be disturbed. Thanks."

"If we're going on," Jerry said, "I'd better call Karen and tell her I'll be a little late. How about we stop at six and you come back to the house for a drink and pick-up supper?"

"Great, if Karen agrees," Lilith said. "We'll have had enough by then. And I could use a drink."

Jerry telephoned, Karen agreed, and Lilith called up the subentry for petty cash.

"Hey, look at that," Jerry said.

Under the heading "Petty Cash" were the identical names, each followed by a comment or two, that he and Lilith had found earlier under "Personal." At the top of the list was MABOY. The comment below it read, "He does not want to admit even to himself that he wants the job. But he does, and Young has raised his hopes. If Snoopy can get something on him, there's a payoff there. But he's as All-American as a Rover boy. Has he ever messed around? Try to find out."

"I think Isabel Doughton was trying to blackmail Tony," Lilith said, "only she had nothing to go on. Can you beat it? She referred to herself in the third person, but with some self-knowledge. 'Snoopy' had a curiosity for profit!"

"It killed the cat," Jerry said, "but I see no reason there to suspect Tony. Snoopy was looking, not threatening."

"MOUND is an eloquent item," Lilith said, reading on. "Note that comment." Jerry did. It said, "MOUND offered $500 for each set of search committee minutes. Snoopy told him $1,000 but settled for $750. He wants to throw a monkey wrench in the works. Hates the King for not admitting his son. Thinks he and MOUTH can take over the place."

"The next entry says more," Jerry commented. It was the comment on MOUTH, and it did say more: "MOUTH is holding out. He talks too much in public. Snoopy knows with whom he's conspiring, so maybe now he'll pay if Snoopy leans hard enough."

"She's blackmailing Humber, or planning to," Lilith said. "We've gone far enough on our own. I'm ready to call Stavros. Humber could have left that candy. This is getting too hot for us to handle alone."

"Don't call yet," Jerry said. "We're not handling the information. We're just obtaining it. Let's get the rest of it and then decide what to do."

"Well, there's not much more," Lilith said, looking at the rest of the page. "PSYCH is clearly Roger Gordon and after his name she has only a question mark. ROMEO is more puzzling."

"Not to me, I'm afraid," Jerry said. "Just read the comment again and use your imagination."

Lilith read it again: "Walking the neighborhood, Snoopy saw ROMEO with a new Juliet. Went back next night. Shades up and curtains pulled back again. He was on top of her. Adultery. What to squeeze him for? He's crazy to be King II."

"Who's that?" Lilith asked.

"From some confidential information I think it's Gene," Jerry replied. "He's been having an affair with Sylvia Wheatley. She told Karen who told me. Hush-hush. I'd just as soon Stavros didn't know."

"We can't not tell him," Lilith said.

"Look," Jerry said. "There's more at the bottom of the page!"

Indeed there was. A last comment with no name preceding it completed the "Petty Cash" file: "Snoopy has him now. Saw R snitch the collar. Held off while thinking about it. Now he can have it all unless Snoopy squeals. So squeeze him hard."

"'R' could stand for so many things," Lilith said. "Robert as in

Robert Humber. Rover as in Rover boy. Roger as in Roger Gordon. Or ROMEO."

"Lil," Jerry said, "I don't like what I have to conclude. On the basis of what we've discovered, 'R' is Gene. Snoopy likes to play with codes. ROMEO stole the collar. She was going to blackmail him, and she surely did. So he poisoned her."

"That looks probable to me, too," Lilith said. "But I find it just about impossible to believe. I'd find it just as hard to believe about Tony or Bob Humber or especially Roger Gordon."

"I agree," Jerry said. "But Gene seems most obvious, so let's just ask him. He's one of my oldest friends. He'll not hurt either of us. Let's talk to him before we tell Stavros what we've found. It's the decent thing to do to a friend."

"The idea makes me very uncomfortable," Lilith objected. "I am, after all a lawyer, and I have a professional obligation not to withhold the kind of information, evidence really, that we've just seen on Isabel's computer. We've gone too far already."

"Lil, at least let me talk to him," Jerry begged. "Then I'll call you. I just can't turn him in, or even report what we've seen, without giving him a chance to explain himself."

Lilith looked hard at Jerry. A long minute passed. "Okay," she then said. "If you promise to call Stavros right after Gene has his say. Only I'm going with you. And I'll call 9-1-1 at the least provocation."

"Thanks," Jerry said. "I owe you a big one. Let's go. I'll leave the car at my house, and we can walk over to Gene's."

Neither Jerry Walsh nor Lilith Furman said a word as Jerry drove the mile or so between the Yale parking lot and his house. He parked his car in the driveway, leaving room for Karen to back out from the garage in case she left the next morning before he did. As he and Lilith opened the car's doors to get out, Karen appeared at the side door of the house. "Hi," she said, "I've been expecting you. It's good to see you Lilith. Come on in. The salad's made and the casserole is in the oven. I'm dying for a drink."

She opened the door, came out, kissed Jerry hello, and then kissed Lilith on the cheek. "You both look funereal," she said. "Why so glum?"

"You had better get inside before you catch cold," Jerry said. "We'll come in for a minute but then we have an urgent errand." They all entered the house and followed Jerry into the kitchen.

"What's so urgent that it can't wait until after we eat?" Karen asked.

Jerry and Lilith looked at each other without replying. "Come on, you two," Karen said. "No secrets from me."

"Look, dear," Jerry said. "We've come across something about the stolen collar that makes it imperative for us to talk to Gene now. We just can't tell you more than that yet. We shouldn't be long, maybe half an hour. Why not turn off the oven, and I'll make you a drink to sip until we return."

"If you say so," Karen said, obviously rather miffed. "But if it's just Gene you want to see, why can't I come along?"

"Better not," Jerry said. Lilith, when Karen then looked quizzically at her, nodded.

"Go right along, then," Karen said. "Never mind the drink. I don't want to detain you." She turned off the oven and left through the swinging door to the dining room.

"You've got to help me make that right later," Jerry said to Lilith. "Now we had better get going. It's about six."

They walked quickly across the street and to the next house but one. Jerry rang the bell. No answer. He rang again. Still no answer. "No one home," Lilith said. "Now let's call Stavros."

"Wait," Jerry said. "Instead let's see whether Gene is at Sylvia's. It's just two more houses and back to our side of the street."

Lilith followed Jerry. He rang Sylvia Wheatley's front door bell. They could hear it buzzing inside the house. They could also hear someone moving about inside. Jerry rang again just as Sylvia opened her door. "Well, hello you two," she said. "What a surprise! Are you selling encyclopedias or have you run out of gin?"

"We're sorry to bother you," Jerry said. "We have to see Gene

Barnard on an urgent matter, and I thought he might be here."

Sylvia hesitated. "I don't know why," she began, stopping after those three words. It seemed to Lilith that Sylvia breathed harder as she added, "Oh dear, you might as well see him then."

Sylvia walked to the bottom of the stairs and called up: "Gene, a couple of friends to see you."

"Who could know to look for me here?" Gene said as he started down the stairs. Sylvia didn't answer. She moved slowly into the living room, went over to the small bar, poured herself a small glass of whiskey, turned, and asked Jerry, Lilith, and Gene, just then entering the room: "Drinks, everyone?"

"Gene," Jerry said, ignoring Sylvia's question, "I'm really sorry about this intrusion. We simply have no choice. We must talk to you at once."

"Jerry, before you do," Lilith interrupted, "tell Sylvia whether you want a drink."

"Yes," Gene said, "whatever it is, have a drink."

"I apologize," Jerry said. "Thank you. Yes, I'd like a vodka martini, on the rocks, please."

"Two, please," Lilith said.

"I'll have some of your single malt Scotch, thanks, Sylvia," Gene said, "and since we're all here, why don't we sit down?" They sat, and Sylvia fixed and passed the drinks. "Now," Gene said, "what is this all about? What could possibly be so important that you two came looking for me here at this hour?"

"Gene," Jerry said, "this is a most unpleasant errand. I have to ask your forgiveness if I've offended you or if I am about to offend you. I came and brought Lilith along because of our long friendship, yours and mine. You probably know that we've been trying to help Fawcett find out who stole the president's collar. Well, only half an hour ago we came across a memo of Isabel Doughton's that makes us think it may have been you. I saw no alternative except to ask you outright. Otherwise we'd have had to go behind your back and report our information to Fawcett and the city police, to that detective, Stavros, who has interviewed you, I know."

Gene said nothing. He seemed to Lilith to be thinking hard. He looked over at Sylvia who smiled at him, went over to his chair and kissed him warmly. "I'm going to leave you to your business," she said, and then disappeared into the front hall.

"See here," Gene said. "Don't be shocked. We love each other. We're going to be married as soon as I'm shed of Betty. I had hoped to keep it all secret but somehow, Jerry, you found out. I wish you'd waited until you could see me somewhere else. This is very hard for Sylvia."

"It's hard for you, too, I'm sure," Jerry said. "And believe me, I hated to invade your privacy. But you see why I had to. Now could you please answer my question?"

Gene sat back, reflecting. "I could tell you that I had nothing to do with the collar," he said at last, "and you're such a good guy that you'd probably believe me. But what the hell! I'm tired of pretending. I've done little but pretend since September. I'm not going to be president, am I Jerry? You and Lilith must know. You might as well tell me."

"No, Gene," Jerry said softly, "you're not."

"Whoever it is will need a new collar," Gene said. "Yes, if you must know, I stole it. On impulse. That's all. It was an idiotic thing to do but I was so damn mad about Shapiro's getting my job, that at that cocktail party, when I saw it sitting there, and no one seemed to be looking, I just plain grabbed it and put it in the poacher's pocket of my tweed jacket. It barely fit. That's the whole story."

"Not quite," Jerry said. "Isabel Doughton saw you and she blackmailed you, so you poisoned her."

"You're out of your bloody mind!" Gene said. "Okay. So she saw me and threatened me. But I'm not damn fool enough to give in to blackmail. She would never have said anything, anyhow, and I couldn't stand the woman. I ignored her note. You should know me well enough to realize I'd never kill anyone. I'm at least that civilized. Now you have offended me, Jerry, and you and your friend, Lilith, can get the hell out."

"I'm afraid we can't without calling the police," Lilith said, moving toward the telephone near the hall.

"For the love of God, woman," Gene shouted at her. "Don't do that. Honestly, I did not poison anyone!"

Lilith hesitated. "Hold it," Jerry said. "We've come this far. Let's hear when else Gene has to say."

"I'm calling Stavros," Lilith said, and she did.

15.

GOOD FOR THE SOUL

They stood there in Sylvia Wheatley's living room, Jerry Walsh and Gene Barnard, listening to Lilith Furman talking to Detective Lieutenant Deno Stavros. "Yes, you heard me," she was saying. "Come at once, as soon as you can, to 11 St. Ronan Terrace. Bring Fawcett if you can. We know who stole the collar. We need you here. And don't use your siren. This is a quiet neighborhood, and I want to keep it so."

"Now that she's done that, what did you mean?" Gene asked Jerry. "What else can I possibly tell you or the cops?" Turning, he addressed Lilith. "Did you think I'd run away? I do make mistakes, Lilith, but at bottom I'm civilized enough so that you did not need the police to shackle me."

"I'm sorry Lilith was impatient," Jerry said. "She's worried. We trust you, or at least I do, but it's been a long day for us. A woman, a Yale employee, has been murdered recently, as you very well know, and Lilith has every right to feel anxious."

"I can speak for myself, Jerry, thank you," Lilith said. "Now as a lawyer and as your friend, Gene, I'm warning you that I'm an officer of the court, that I do not represent you, that Jerry cannot represent you, and that anything you say can be used as evidence against you. You are entitled to…"

At that point, Gene laughed and interrupted. "Listen to her," he said to Jerry, "she's telling me my Miranda rights. Come off it, Lil, I know they'll punish me for taking the collar. I already said it was a dumb impulse. Relax. Have another drink and we'll wait for your troops."

"You can stop laughing," Lilith replied. "This isn't funny. I'll be glad to wait for Stavros, but you had better realize that you're the obvious one to have poisoned Isabel Doughton."

"Poison Isabel! Don't be foolish. We grew up together right here in New Haven. She was in my older sister's class at the old Day-Prospect Hill School. She's a pig, always been a pain in the derriere, but it never occurred to me to kill her. Anyway poison, Lil, as you should know from Catherine de Medici, is a woman's weapon. Jerry will attest that I'm a male jock."

"Tell it to Stavros," Lilith said.

They all stood silently for what seemed to her an eternity. Then the bell rang, Stavros opened the front door, which had not been locked, and he and Fawcett walked in, both of them with police automatics in hand.

"Here we are, Miss Furman," he said. "What's going on?"

"You don't need your guns," Lilith replied, "but I'm very glad to see you."

Sylvia, who had gone upstairs to her bedroom, had heard the front door bell ring and looked out the window. She had seen the police cruiser and come downstairs. Now she entered the living room, looked around, and said, "Is this convention open to anyone, or should I leave again?"

"Sylvia," Lilith said, "these officers are Chief Fawcett from the Yale police and Detective Stavros of the city. I called them. Gene has confessed to stealing the president's collar, and I felt we needed an official presence. I regret having to summon strangers to your home."

"I see," Sylvia said. "Why don't you come into the kitchen with me, Lilith, while the men get on with their duties." Briefly Lilith hesitated. She did not want to be left out, but she vehemently disliked guns. She nodded to Sylvia and the two women left.

"Now let's have the story," Stavros said.

Jerry explained that he and Lilith had guessed the code word for Doughton's computer files, accessed some files, examined them, and found evidence that she had been trying to use information she had gathered for blackmail. "She was trying to extort money from Dean Robert Humber, we concluded, and from Professor Barnard. She had seen him take the president's collar. Lilith and I suspect he probably poisoned Isabel Doughton, but he's an old friend, and I wanted to ask him to his face before we called you. He's admitted his guilt about the collar, but he denies poisoning anyone. Lilith decided it was time to let you know."

"Goddamn it, Walsh, I could take you in for obstruction of justice, and I just might," Stavros shouted, livid with anger. "Who the hell do you think you are? Holmes and Watson?" he continued, now more quietly. "Nice of you to let us in on your little secret. Don't you understand we're dealing with a murder? Can't you get that through your blue brain? How nice of you to bring us here and to let us in on your news. I wanted your help. I didn't commission you deputy sheriffs."

"Easy, Deno," Fawcett said. "They've done pretty well, and nothing is lost."

"Where's the collar, for a starter?" Stavros asked.

"I thought it prudent to get rid of it," Gene said, "so I sold it to a dealer in East Haven who buys gold. I'd sold him my old wedding ring when Betty left—she was my wife, Detective Stavros. He gave me the dollar equivalent of the collar's weight in gold plus something for the jewels. But he's surely melted it down by now. You could ask. Carmen Negretti, The Second Chance Shop, just off Interstate 95, down about a block from the airport exit."

"I'm going to have to take you in," Stavros said, "as a suspect in the murder of Isabel Doughton."

"Do as you think you must," Gene said. "But you may be sued for false arrest. I tell you, I did not do it. You have the wrong man."

"Look, buster," Stavros exploded, "I've got you for a felony that should ruin you at Yale forever, so don't give me your snotty crap. As far as murder goes, any cop would book you on suspicion."

Barnard opened his mouth to reply but Jerry quickly broke in. "Gene, Gene, shut up until you have a lawyer."

"He's right," Stavros said. "I'll read you your rights. But hold up a minute. Professor Walsh, you saw that computer stuff I've yet to see. Can Miss Furman get it to me, or is that too much to ask?"

"Yes, of course," Jerry replied, "but only, as I understand it, after she can print out what you want. One thing more. As I said, Professor Barnard is my friend. He's also not the only possible suspect. Doughton was after Dean Humber, too, and maybe Tony Celotto. And one of them could have left those chocolates. Either of them could have bought the candy. So go easy on Professor Barnard. You just might have the wrong man."

"I think Professor Walsh is right," Fawcett said. "We still can't be sure who poisoned the woman. And Yale has yet to bring charges about the collar, though that may well be done. So be careful, Deno."

"Thank you for your votes of confidence," Gene said. "Jerry, please call a lawyer for me. Mine handles only divorces, and my former lawyer was Dray who doesn't suit me on this matter."

"Come on along, Barnard," Stavros said. "All you Yalies talk too much. My guess is you're guilty as hell."

Just then, Lilith, who had appeared in the kitchen doorway, called out, "Wait!"

The men stared at her. She looked ashen. "Wait," she repeated, "Sylvia has something to say."

Earlier, when she had entered the kitchen, Sylvia had gone at once to the sink, drawn herself a glass of water, moved then to a cupboard against the east wall, and opened its door. She withdrew an envelope and a box. She poured the contents of the envelope into the glass and swallowed the mixture. Smiling at Lilith, she offered her the box which she was now uncovering. "Have one," she said. "They're very good and wholly safe."

Lilith looked into the box. To her disbelief, it held chocolate-covered cherries. Startled, she looked hard at Sylvia. "Go ahead," Sylvia said, "these aren't poisoned."

"What did you say?" Lilith asked, now alarmed.

"These are not poisoned," Sylvia repeated. "The others were."

"Sylvia," Lilith said, "are you telling me something awful?"

"I poisoned Isabel Doughton, if that's what you mean," Sylvia said calmly. "It's time to confess. Gene has had enough, and he had nothing to do with the poison. He didn't even know about it, for that matter, still doesn't. It was entirely my idea and my doing."

"Back up," Lilith said. "How could you have known about TTX? How could you have obtained it? Why would you have picked on the Doughton woman, and how did you put the chocolates on her desk?"

"Gene and I have been lovers for some time," Sylvia said. "He means more to me than life itself. To my delight, he has come to tell me everything he does, his every thought. It's been marvelous to share his life. I've never before known anyone like Gene, never before loved anyone so much. So I knew everything because he told me. He told me about his committee and how it went to see the TTX in the lab where doctors had used it in important experiments. He told me where the lab was. I did not forget what he said. And then, weeping, he told me later about how Shapiro was offered the job Gene deserved. You know, in some ways he's rather like a child, and I'm older than he. He expects things to go his way. Like the child I never had. But he's also a wonderful lover. Later still he told me about the reception in the secretary's office and about his uncontrolled impulse. I wanted to protect him, to save him for myself. So when he told me about the blackmail note, from Snoopy, he said, but he knew it had to be the Doughton woman, he also told me he wasn't going to pay her. So I simply killed her to keep her from talking."

"Sylvia," Lilith said, "are you making all this up?"

"You better believe, as they say, because I'm telling you the whole truth."

"How did you obtain the poison, then, and where did you buy the candy?"

"I walked into the lab and took the poison from its shelf. It was labeled. No one noticed me. And I bought the candy at my drug store, the Country Club Pharmacy. The girl at the counter scarcely noticed me. I bought two boxes, one in case I made a mistake. But I injected the TTX without trouble. You could really eat one of the cherries if you wanted to. I had more than enough poison, enough to keep in case of an emergency. I just swallowed the rest. And it was easy enough to walk into Isabel Doughton's office and leave the candy for her. No one was there. She was so greedy that she probably ate it on the spot. Served her right. Gene couldn't take her seriously. But I did. Now you better call the others. I'm beginning to feel woozy."

Lilith had been incredulous while Sylvia was talking. She suddenly realized what Sylvia had said. "Oh my God," Lilith said," we have to get you some help!"

"Too late," Sylvia said. "But I want to see Gene and tell him I love him. And I'd better tell the others he didn't do it."

It was then that Lilith had entered the living room.

Sylvia had followed her. "Gene, darling," she now said. "Please come hold me. I swallowed quite a bit of TTX several minutes ago and it's beginning to work. I poisoned that dreadful woman. You knew nothing about it. She deserved to die. Now so do I. But always remember that I love you. We were wonderful for each other. I hate to leave."

Lilith ran to the phone to call an ambulance while both Gene and Stavros started toward Sylvia, Gene keening as he moved. "Don't," she said. "Don't hurt me. It's getting hard to talk. Take me up to bed, dear, and embrace me there. It won't be long."

"Stay right where you are. Both of you," Stavros warned, his gun pointed toward Gene. "You're both under arrest. Fawcett, you make sure an ambulance and doctor are on their way."

Ignoring Stavros, Gene took Sylvia in his arms and raced up the stairs while the others watched, horrified. Stavros, furious, fired one warning shot into the ceiling and chased after them.

"Oh, let them go," Lilith shouted at him. "He's taking her up to die." They heard a door slam on the second floor and a lock click.

"Damn!" Stavros said. "You should know this is bad procedure, Miss Furman. I'm staying right here for two minutes and then I'm going after them. While we're waiting, suppose you tell us the whole story. You can repeat it later for a police stenographer. Don't hold back or so help me I'll take you and Walsh downtown. I want it right now."

While Chief Fawcett and Jerry listened, speechless still, Lilith, her story punctuated by bursts of tears, told Stavros all that Sylvia had told her.

Sylvia died while the rescue crew was moving her to the ambulance. Gene had followed them downstairs but Stavros, barring the door, warned him not to leave the house. "Nobody leaves!" Stavros said. "I want a full account from everyone here. Everything, from the beginning. You can go into the kitchen one by one and talk to me and the officer who's just pulling up outside. Fawcett will see that otherwise you stay in the living room. Okay, Chief?

"Glad to help," Fawcett said, "but may they use the phone?"

"Yeah," Stavros said. "Barnard may want a lawyer before he confesses officially."

"I need to call my wife," Jerry said. "And I'd like your permission also to call President Stiles to tell him what's happened."

"Fawcett," Stavros said, "you can let them use the phone so long as no one leaves. You want a lawyer, Barnard?"

Gene turned toward Stavros, said nothing, turned then toward Jerry and looked at him pleadingly. To Jerry, he seemed almost in a catatonic state.

"He's not fit to make any statement or decision now," Jerry said to Stavros who was beckoning to the policeman who walked in the door. "Give him some time. Lilith can dictate to the tape recorder your officer has in his hands while I try to get through to Gene."

"He's right," Fawcett said.

"Okay," Stavros said. "Professor Furman, you come with me. I'll get to you next, Walsh, and then to Barnard."

Jerry led Gene to a chair, called Karen to say he and Lilith were detained by a new development in the case they were investigating, then called Charley Dray to ask him quickly to send a competent criminal lawyer to Sylvia Wheatley's house to advise Professor

Barnard about his rights. The urgency in Jerry's voice precluded any discussion.

"Gene," Jerry then said, gently, "do you want to tell me anything I don't know before I call the King?"

Gene, his grief seemingly palpable, stared numbly at Jerry. Then, as if shaking off a trance, he muttered, "It was an impulse. I was too far gone to realize what I was doing."

That reply exhausted Jerry's patience. "Damn you, Gene," he said. "I suppose it was another impulse that kept you from returning the collar during the days after you stole it. And another impulse that persuaded you that you could still become president."

His attention caught, Gene glared back at Jerry who continued, his voice rising. "You've forgotten the difference between right and wrong, if you ever knew it. Worse, you've been using our friendship, playing me for a sucker. I've supported you again and again, but your critics were right. You're a lightweight. You don't come within miles of what's needed in a Yale president. And you're a thief. I'm going to urge the King to put you behind bars."

Fully alert now, and provoked by Jerry's outburst, Gene shook his head and spoke up. "That's your problem," he said. "I don't care what you do or what the King does. Don't you preach to me! You're Stiles' toady and everybody knows it. With Sylvia gone, there's not much left in my life, which is something that, with your cheap moralism, you can't begin to understand. But you can tell your pal the King that if he doesn't charge me with theft, I'll resign at once, get in this term's grades, and get the hell out of this place. Maybe to Rome where I can breathe antiquity. Maybe to the University of Tasmania, which is advertising for a classicist, so my course assistant tells me. God knows that should be far enough for you and Stiles. You've been too loyal a friend, Jerry, and I suppose I am a thief. But I'm tired of friends who teach at Yale. I'm sick of the whole place. Go call your King and tell him whatever you like."

Jerry, stunned in his turn, asked Fawcett to watch over Gene while he called President Stiles. The King heard him out but decided at once to avoid the publicity that the prosecution of Gene Barnard would have entailed. He would hold Barnard to his terms. Tasmania, the King remarked, was just about as close to Eugene Barnard as he ever wanted again to be. He added that he would privately bring Proxmire Young and Dick Mason up to date.

Karen Walsh had been irritated when Jerry and Lilith went off without her to call on Gene Barnard. Her irritation changed to anxiety when she heard the grim tone of Jerry's voice on the telephone telling her they would be detained. She threw an old, brown cardigan across her shoulders and left her house intending to walk over to Gene's. But she saw police cruisers outside of Sylvia's house, and she headed that way just as an ambulance reached St. Ronan Terrace. Her anxiety rising, Karen stopped while the ambulance passed her and the rescue crew entered Sylvia's front door. Then she ran after them. She looked beyond the door, now standing open, and could just see the rescue crew examining Sylvia. It was obvious from their postures and motions that her dear friend was dead. Stifling a scream, Karen retreated a few steps and waited while the rescue crew carried out Sylvia's body. The door shut behind them.

Shocked into immobility, Karen stood, slumped, near the police cruisers. She could not imagine what had happened to Sylvia or what might have happened to Jerry or Lilith. After what seemed to her an eternity, though it was less than five minutes, Lilith, sobbing, emerged from the house. The two women fell into each other's arms. Jerry, who followed Lilith almost immediately, embraced them both and gently guided them home. Once there, Karen and Lilith began to quiet down. Jerry offered them some brandy, which they took and sipped. "What…" Karen began, but before she could finish her question, Lilith, drawing a deep breath, told her that Sylvia had confessed to poisoning Isabel Doughton and then poisoned herself.

During supper, Lilith and Jerry gave Karen a quick account of their afternoon of surprise and horror. The three agreed to plan a memorial service for Sylvia. Lilith would see to the music. Karen would prepare a eulogy. Jerry, a forgiving man, suggested that Gene Barnard should deliver another. Both women objected. Gene's selfish ambition and jealous impulsiveness, they agreed, had created the circumstances that brought about Sylvia's death. They did not want him even to attend the service. "All that charm, all that intelligence and all that talent," Lilith said, "obscured the egotism that moved him. He drove his wife to leave him and drove his beloved to the grave."

"Perhaps, Jerry suggested, "that's punishment enough."

"No," Karen said firmly. "The King is letting him off the hook, but we need not."

As it worked out, Gene left Yale and New Haven on a flight to Rome the next weekend, never to return. Jerry later heard that he reached Tasmania in time to teach during the June semester. Tony Celotto arranged a private burial for Isabel Doughton. At the services for Sylvia, attended by her many friends, Karen spoke and so did Martha Mason who had come to know Sylvia well while she was painting the Masons' daughter's portrait. Both of them talked about Sylvia's artistic talent, her gentleness, her love of children, her humane nature.

Those were admirable qualities, Lilith remarked to Karen and Jerry as they left the church, but love as ardent as Sylvia's had made for murder.

"Why do you think so?" Karen asked.

"Because she loved Gene not only as her man," Lilith replied, "but also as if he had been her child, and a mother's love can turn deadly if she thinks her child is in peril."

"You're right," Jerry said. "There's nothing love won't do. The ancient Greeks knew all about that."

Deno Stavros would not have put it that way, but he would have agreed.

Printed in the United States
34596LVS00004B/67-72